Broken Realm
The New Age

Autumn A. Hutchings

Green Ivy Publishing
1 Lincoln Centre
18W140 Butterfield Road
Suite 1500
Oakbrook Terrace IL 60181-4843
www.greenivybooks.com

ISBN: 978-1-945379-13-0

*This book is dedicated to my father
David C. Hutchings*

*He was my biggest supporter and always
believed that this story would succeed.*

I love you dad, you will always be missed.

*A big thank you to the ones who helped start
this whole thing,*

Matt, Lexi, Cano and of course Bridget.

*Thank you, without you I would have never had
the idea for this story.*

Table Of Contents

CHAPTER ONE:

Deadville

Every day, I stare out the window of my bedroom and look out at the small town I am forced to live in. I'm eighteen, waiting just to graduate and leave this place. It's simple, isn't it? To me, it's no different than every other pathetic life that lives in this world right along with me. It's boring. I want more to life than this; I need more.

I live in a town named Leadville in the state of Colorado. It's the typical mountain town, which is surrounded by a vast green forest of pine trees. At least, I think they're pine trees. Let's just say that my lack of entertainment in this place kills me. Don't get me wrong. This town isn't so bad, but it's still very dull—almost dead. I'd go mad if it weren't for my friends, Bridget and Griffin, the Knight siblings. They always have my back, and we're never apart. I guess

I wouldn't be able to survive without my little sister, Lexi, either since she's pretty great.

"Mason! Get down here right now!" Ariel yelled from the kitchen.

Ariel was my legal guardian. I've been with her as long as I could remember. She isn't exactly the best person. I slowly made my way downstairs, not excited at all. I entered the kitchen, not really focusing on anything due to the fact that I was tired from a long day at school. I stood at the doorway and looked right at the dark-haired woman who was glaring in my direction.

I sighed. I knew I was in trouble just by looking at her. "What do you want?" I asked.

She didn't relax and kept her eyes fixed on me. I felt awkward, fidgeting under her glare. I hated it when people looked at me as if they were angry with me.

"Your school called just now," Ariel said blankly.

My heart started beating a little faster. I really didn't know why. But you know that feeling you get when you did something wrong? That's what I was feeling. I was feeling the fear of getting in trouble for being a bad kid.

Ariel rested her hand on the counter and her other hand on her hip. "Did you really set loose a raccoon at school?!" she questioned with an angry tone.

I sighed, "I swear it wasn't my idea, nor did I actually do it."

I really didn't do it. Bridget did. I just watched. Bridget thought it would be a funny senior prank to release a thousand crickets into the school. I objected and convinced her to tone it down a bit, so she did. Bridget ended up, somehow, managing to capture a raccoon and let it roam free in our school, Lake County High. Since I was a witness, or in their eyes an accomplice, I got in trouble too. Hence, the phone call.

"They want to suspend you, Mason," Ariel stated.

"That's their problem," I said. I was beginning to zone out, and believe me, when I zone out, I get stupid.

"Mason Haining, I swear if you don't stop being a smart ass, I will send you six feet under!" Ariel snapped.

I hated it when she got this way. I also hated it when she called me Mason Haining. Sure, she may have adopted me, but I didn't like her and didn't want her last name. I just went by Mason.

"Look. I'm sorry. I won't do it again," I said even though I didn't do anything.

Ariel was about to speak when Lexi, my sister, walked in, and Ariel got distracted. "Oh, Lexi, I didn't know you were home," Ariel said as she turned and faced my younger sister.

Lexi opened the fridge, pulled out a can of root beer, and popped it open. "I just got here. Opening the door and hearing you two fighting made me realize *again* how much I hated being home because that's all you two ever do," she remarked.

Ariel rolled her eyes at Lexi. With her focus off me, I slowly backed out of the room and fled out the front door only to hear, *"Mason!!!"* in the background as I slammed the door and ran to my car. I reached for my keys, and my heart sank when I realized they were still in the house. Kicking the car tire, I realized I couldn't go back in, so I just darted up the street before Ariel went outside the house. I headed toward the woods just north of my street. Sometimes, I would go there to escape. I descended into the vast pine tree forest and trekked through the woods as the dead pine needles crunched beneath my every step.

I made my way to a clearing in the woods where I spent most of my days just to think. Sometimes, Bridget and Griffin would join me, and we would simply hang out here. This was my getaway—well— the closest I could get to a getaway. This place did make me a bit uneasy. I always felt as if I were being watched. I know that I was being paranoid, but it was a feeling I could never shake. Once I reached the center of the clearing, I lay down and stared up at the sky as the tall, green grass that looked like a type of wheat surrounded me, flowing with the gentle breeze. I watched the clouds cover the sun, giving me shade. It looked as though it was going to rain any moment, but that didn't bother me. I'd rather stay out in the rain than go home.

"Mason, I swear. If you make me chase you out here ever again, I will hurt you."

I heard a voice a few feet away from me, and sadly, I recognized it. I rolled my eyes and sat up. "Go away, Lexi." I glared at my little sister who had walked up to me and plopped down on the ground beside me.

"Why did you leave me alone with Ariel like that?" she asked.

"Because she was yelling at me, and I wanted to leave," I explained.

"I know you and Ariel don't get along, but running off like that isn't going to help anything," she told me.

Like I didn't know that already. But I planned to move out as soon as I could. Bridget and I already had it all planned out. Since her and Griffin's dad was a drunk and their mother left them when they were babies, they only had each other and me. We all planned on living together after Bridget and I graduated. Griffin already dropped out of school, so that wouldn't be a problem for him. I didn't need Ariel. I didn't need anyone but Bridget and Griffin. But as I looked at my sister, I knew I needed her too. And I couldn't leave her behind.

I let out a sigh, "Lexi, can we not talk about this?"

"Fine," she intoned. "Why don't we talk about you? Are you okay? You seemed pretty down for the past week. Maybe even before that too."

I looked her right in the eyes. "I'm fine," I lied.

Lexi kept quiet for a while, looking at the ground. "I'm sorry. I'm just really worried," she stated. "You seem to get angrier every day. I see you when you think I'm not looking or when you think no one's looking. You look desolate," Lexi expressed.

It made me kind of embarrassed, worrying my sixteen-year-old sister. I didn't want her to be worried about me because she didn't need that added burden. What made it worse was that she was right. I couldn't help but feel alone. I would wake up every morning and think. What was the point of me? Why was I born just to suffer in life like this? Everything went wrong in my life, and I couldn't remember the last time I was happy. Truly happy. The days just grew longer and less bearable, and all I could do was hope that things would get better eventually. All I had was hope, but even that was starting to fade away.

"Please don't worry about me," I begged, not looking at Lexi.

She got up and held her hand out to me. "Come on. Let's go home. It looks like it's about to rain," she said.

I took her hand and stood up.

We went back into the forest, and even with the tree tops covering us, I still felt little raindrops plop on me every once in a while. Lexi was a few feet ahead of me. She appeared lost in her head as she always seemed to be when she was worried about something. I felt bad for making her worry, so I had to start being more happy even if I really wasn't. I couldn't do this to her anymore. I let out a sigh. Now that I thought about it, I seemed to do that a lot.

I began to feel paranoid again, having that same feeling of something watching me. I turned my head slightly to the left and almost had a heart attack. Something was behind me, a black figure in the distance. I spun around to its direction, but it was gone. Confused, I stared at the spot where the figure had stood. I swear I saw something. It was something black, a figure that appeared as man but different. And the eyes...piercing, glowing, yellow eyes viciously staring at me. I was starting to go nuts. I knew it.

"Hey, Mason, come on. Stopping isn't going to get us home any faster."

"Right. Sorry," I said and just shook it off as I ran to catch up to Lexi.

When we got home, something had happened, something odd. We walked into the living room, and there was a strange man sitting on our couch with a beer in hand. Ariel was sitting in a chair by him, actually smiling. Lexi and I stopped in our tracks and just stared at the man with onyx black hair and tan skin. He wore a black, leather jacket, black jeans, and biker boots. He looked pretty scary.

Ariel, still smiling at the stranger, glanced at Lexi and me. "Oh, this is Mason and Lexi."

He got up and walked toward us, holding out his hand to me with a smile. "Hey, I'm Matt."

I rejected Matt's handshake and looked plainly at him in disapproval. What the hell was this? When did Ariel meet a guy? And when did a guy actually like Ariel?

"Okay, then," Matt said and turned to Lexi. "You must be Lexi. Like I said, I'm Matt. It's nice to meet you."

He was oddly polite for a guy who wore a leather jacket and had a lot of skull rings. I noticed Ariel was glaring at me. I could tell she wanted me to be nice to him, but why bother when I didn't care?

Lexi smiled a bit at him. "It's nice to meet you too. Are you a friend of Ariel's?" she questioned. Lexi was obviously the smart one and knew that getting information was more important than being a rude, anti-social jerk like me. I tend to forget that.

"Yes, sort of. We're dating," Matt stated. "Did she not tell you?"

"She didn't mention anything about a guy," Lexi said with a smile that looked so fake that she could be on a commercial selling dish detergent or some brand of gum. "I've never seen you around town before. Are you new here?"

"Yeah, moved here a few weeks ago," Matt said.

Ariel walked up to Matt and grabbed his hand. "Sorry I didn't tell you guys. I just didn't know how," she said. She was shorter than Matt. Ariel was actually a few inches shorter than me, so Matt being pretty damn tall skyrocketed over her make me feel like a midget. I was 5'9", and I swore he looked like a giant. Okay, that's an exaggeration. But you get the point.

"Well, you could have just said, Hey, Mason, Hey, Lexi... Um, I found a new boyfriend. He's really creepy looking and probably murdered someone recently," I sassed.

"Mason," Ariel snapped aggressively.

My hands shot up in mock surrender. "Sorry. I have no filter sometimes."

Matt just laughed a little, "Don't worry. He's just being the man of the house."

"Not really. I just don't like you," I said.

"Mason!" Ariel then shouted.

I looked at Lexi with a look of anxiety. Ariel was going to murder me. Lexi just held back a laugh.

Matt nodded. "Understandable. The feeling is somewhat mutual."

I glared. "Good."

Ariel tightened her jaw and clenched her fist. "He's so lucky I haven't kicked him out yet."

"I've been begging you to kick me out since I got here," I continued my snarky comments. I was on a roll, probably not for the best, but I was bad at first impressions. No, that's not quite it…um I'm bad at life. Yeah, there it is. I'm bad at life. I hated almost everything especially meeting new people. And my bitter hatred for the world and everyone in it besides my best friends and my little sister just made me a little shit.

"Well, this just got awkward," Matt commented.

"Just?" Lexi chuckled.

"Matt and I are going to a movie now. I'll see you both in the morning," Ariel said, heading for the door.

Matt looked at us. "Once again, it was very nice to meet you, Lexi...Mason." He gave us a tiny smile and a nod, looked at us for a bit, then walked over to Ariel who already got her jacket on ready to get out of here.

"Dinner is whatever you two find," she said as she walked out.

Matt gave us a little wave and followed, closing the door behind him.

I glared at the beer bottle on the coffee table, hoping that this guy was just a phase for Ariel. Lexi walked over to the kitchen, and I decided to tag along since I was getting kind of hungry.

"So, why were you so rude to Matt?" Lexi asked as she opened a cabinet, pulling out a box of Kellogg's Fruity Pebbles cereal and pouring it into a bowl.

I shrugged. I really didn't have a reason, which kind of made me feel bad now but only a little. "Does it matter?" I responded with a question.

She glanced at me as she put milk in her bowl. "Not really, but he didn't seem so bad... In fact, he actually seemed a little familiar. Don't you think?"

"No, why would you say that?" I asked.

Lexi took a bite of the Fruity Pebbles. "I don't know," she mumbled with her mouth full.

"It's probably your mind playing tricks on you. I'm going to bed now," I told her, heading for the stairs. "I'm tired."

"Goodnight," she called out to me as I left.

Once I got up to my room, I crashed onto my bed, not even bothering to change my clothes. I stared up at my ceiling, thinking. Lexi was right. Something about Matt seemed familiar now that I thought about it. Why though? I've never met him before, and I would've remembered meeting someone like that. Things gradually seemed to get more and more complicated. Here I was with that same gut feeling I always had, something that told me I didn't belong here. I never had, and I believed that. But honestly, does anyone?

CHAPTER TWO:

The Lake

After contemplating life, I awoke the next morning. That Matt guy probably thought I was a snotty jerk now, not that I cared what he thought of me. Honestly though, I didn't want someone else in my life who was going to disappoint me again. I was sick of being let down. Letting out a sigh, I slipped out of my blue sheets and crashed on the floor. Slowly, I tried to get up, but my laziness bested me. I was lying on the floor for a while until I heard a knock on my window. I turned my gaze up toward it to find Bridget and Griffin waving at me. Bridget motioned me to open the window as Griffin kept his big goofy smile on. I was finally able to get up—now that I had the motivation to. I unlocked the window and cracked it open, so they could crawl into my room.

"Hey, guys," I greeted my friends.

"What's up?" Griffin asked as he hopped into the room with his sister. He then plopped right onto my bed, making himself at home.

"Nothing much. I just found out some random guy named Matt is now dating Ariel. It's weird. I'm pretty sure this is how horror movies start," I told them.

"Wait. You're kidding, right?" Bridget questioned.

"Sadly, no. Just watch. He's going to be a serial killer," I said.

Laughing, Bridget patted my head as she walked to my desk and started messing with things. She and I were both eighteen unlike Griffin who was seventeen. However, Griffin was more mature than Bridget and me, which said a lot about us.

Griffin looked directly at me. His light brown hair was all messed up from my pillows. "Well, maybe this guy is exactly what this house needs. What if he's a decent human being who just wants to fall in love and help raise two beautiful teenage girls?"

When he said that, I threw the first thing I grabbed, hitting him right in the stomach. Unfortunately for him, that object was my history textbook. He groaned as it landed.

Bridget laughed, "Although he insulted you, Griffin has a point. At least, give the guy a chance. If he really is that bad of a guy, we'll put bats in his car or something." Bridget smiled.

"Where would you even get the bats?" Griffin asked her.

She shrugged. "I'm sure I'll figure it out."

Bridget and Griffin may have been siblings, but they didn't look much alike. In fact, Bridget looked more like me than she did Griffin. We almost looked like twins. Bridget and I had the same dark chocolate brown hair and the same porcelain skin. But we had different eye colors with mine being a light shade of blue. People always told me that they could stop anyone in their tracks because they were so fascinating. Bridget had an odd shade of cyan eyes unlike any I have ever seen. They looked almost alien although I wasn't going to judge.

My eyes were pretty abnormal too. As for Griffin, he had emerald green eyes and an olive skin tone. He was also pretty skinny. Bridget honestly looked like a goddess. All the guys at school wanted to date her, and all the girls were jealous of her. Then there was me, who just saw her as a sister.

I always felt like I was her unpopular friend until one day I found out there was a group of girls at our school calling themselves the Mason Fan Club. Since I was the only Mason at the school, I kind of figured it was me. Then they started following me to places, and it got creepy. Griffin was pretty good-looking himself, so we were all attractive people. We just stuck together and let people admire us from afar—as conceited as that sounds.

"So, did you guys come over for a reason or just because?" I asked.

Out of the blue, Bridget poked me and skipped out of the room. She was probably off to go and antagonize Lexi or find a snake to put in Ariel's toilet. If she did, I wasn't going to stop her.

"Danny's drunk again," Griffin stated. He sat up, letting out a small sigh and looking upset. "I really hate him."

Danny was an alcoholic, who was also Bridget and Griffin's father. It seemed as though all he did was sleep and drink beer. I haven't even seen him get up to go to the bathroom before. Maybe he wore a diaper. Plus, Danny seems to pick favorites with his kids. Bridget was the golden child, and Griffin was the loser that he would smack around for fun. That made me hate him even more. I didn't want to make assumptions, but Griffin didn't look anything like his dad. I always thought that maybe Griffin wasn't really Danny's son.

Once, I almost got in a fist fight with the guy, but Bridget stopped us before any punches were thrown. I just couldn't help but feel the need to take care of Griffin, who only had Bridget and me. When Griffin was 13, he got into some pretty bad things, namely drugs. I really only talked Bridget then, not him. One night when I was walking home from a school play I had been in, I found him on the street alone and crying.

Danny kicked him out, and Bridget wasn't allowed to go with him. Believe me; she wanted to. I couldn't just leave him there, so I took him home with me and let him spend the night. Griffin and I had been friends ever since, and I supported his efforts to get sober. He's the strongest person I have ever met. Luckily, Bridget never got into those things, so she was a happy little ray of sunshine with a dark side.

"Well, you guys can stay here as long as you want. I'm sure Danny won't notice," I told Griffin, giving him a slight smile.

He smiled back.

"Okay, I'm going to get dressed. You can go wait for me with Bridget and Lexi," I said.

"What? I can't watch?" Griffin joked.

I gave him a weird look. "As much as I love you man, no."

"All right," he laughed, heading out of my room.

I shut the door behind him and quickly got ready for the day. I went downstairs after I combed my hair into my usual skater-like style and threw on my favorite band t-shirt, My Chemical Romance. I wore black jeans and converse, and to top it all off, I threw on my lucky white Vans jacket.

"Mason, I made breakfast!" Bridget beamed and showed me a plate of chocolate chip pancakes.

Lexi walked over to her and chuckled a bit, "Actually, I made them, but she did flip a few pancakes for me."

I laughed and walked over to the table and sat by Griffin. With the help of Bridget, Lexi has made a wonderful breakfast. Lexi made chocolate chip pancakes and scrambled eggs with bacon. She had Bridget make apple juice. I poured myself a glass before handing the pitcher to Griffin. I chugged down the juice and began to eat my pancakes. For being sixteen, Lexi was pretty damn good at cooking.

We were all having a wonderful breakfast together. It was one of those moments that made you happy to be alive and to be with the ones you love most. But of course, Ariel came in and interrupted us.

"Mason, Lexi!" she sang. "I have something to tell you." Ariel walked over to the dining room, smiling. "So, you both seemed a little upset about Matt, so he came up with a plan to bond more with you two."

"Eww," was all I had to say to that.

"Pass," Lexi said and took a bite of her bacon.

Ariel frowned. "You didn't even listen to what he has planned."

"Okay. What does he have planned?" Lexi asked.

"He wants to take you guys camping at Turquoise Lake," she stated.

"Hell no!" I shouted.

"I'd rather not," Lexi remarked.

Ariel pouted. For a woman who was at least thirty, she sure acted like a teenage girl. I think she needed a wakeup call.

"Come on guys. Give him a chance," Bridget interrupted. "He might be a nice person."

"Yeah, give him a chance," Griffin said.

"See! Your friends think you should do it," Ariel expressed.

I rolled my eyes and shot a look at Bridget and Griffin. "My friends are idiots."

"Speak for yourself," Bridget commented.

Griffin chuckled, and they high-fived.

"Mason, if you don't go, you are grounded for a week. No friends. No TV. No computer or Wi-Fi," Ariel said.

I turned to her and gasped, gazing at her in utter horror. No Wi-Fi?! How was I going to live?! She was really laying down the law this time.

"And Lexi," Ariel continued, "If you don't go, then you are grounded for four days. No Wi-Fi, no TV, and no friends."

"Why do I get grounded longer?!" I complained.

"Because you were an asshole to Matt last night," Ariel said.

"He deserved it," I said.

"Yeah, he probably did," Griffin said. For some reason, Bridget smacked him. "I mean, no he didn't," he uttered.

"How about this? Go with us to Turquoise lake, and you can bring your friends," Ariel said to me.

"Sounds fun. I'm up for it." Bridget smiled.

"So am I," Griffin said.

"Ugh, okay. Fine. I'll go..." I muttered with irritation.

Lexi sighed, "Count me in."

Ariel smiled like an idiot and hugged Lexi. She knew I'd kill her if she touched me, so she didn't bother. "Thank you so much! He's taking us next Saturday, so be ready by then." She practically danced to her room.

I didn't get why she cared so much about that guy anyway. He seemed like a dirt bag to me.

"So...what should we do today?" Bridget asked once Ariel was gone.

"We could go get some ice cream," Lexi suggested.

"Yes!" Bridget cheered and shot up.

But Griffin stopped her.

"Um, Bridget, we haven't finished breakfast yet," I told her.

She sat back down, pouting a little as Lexi and Griffin giggled.

After all of us finally finished our breakfast, Bridget and Lexi went out to get ice cream from the local ice cream shop, D'love Gourmet Coffee and Ice Cream. If you haven't gotten ice cream from D'love, then you haven't lived. It's heaven—and their coffee is pretty great too. Griffin and I waited at home for them to come back with the ice cream. We went outside to the pond in the backyard. Griffin was looking at his phone, and from his expression, it looked like something was wrong.

"You okay, dude?" I asked him.

Griffin sighed and showed me his phone. I was appalled at what I read on the screen. Griffin's father was sending him horrible texts. It read, *I hate you, and you're a worthless piece of shit.* And much worse... I could feel the rage flood into me. Who the hell did this guy think he was?

"This is not okay!" I shouted. "The guy gets drunk all day, makes you and your sister pay the bills and shit, and treats you like you aren't important?! You are important, Griffin. Don't listen to this asshole."

He put his face in his hands and didn't look at me.

"You aren't worthless, Griffin. He's a low-life scumbag. You're awesome. And Bridget, Lexi, and I love you. He's just an asshole." I didn't care how much effort it took. He had to know how important he was—not just to me but to the world. He had to know he was here for a reason. "People are going to try to bring you down. You have to forget them and know that they don't deserve you. No matter how bad you feel or how alone you may think, you're never alone. And there's always tomorrow. I'm always here, man. I'm always here for you."

Right then, I felt his phone buzz, so I checked it. Danny texted him once again.

Answer me, you little bastard.

Then, I did something I sort of regret. Actually, scratch that. I called Danny, put the phone up to my ear, and listened to its ring. I waited to hear the man's drunken and vile voice. When he picked up, I clenched my teeth as I listened to Danny's spiel.

"You worthless child, you should've answered your phone an hour ago. Where are you and your sister? Tell me now, or next time I see you, I'll beat your ass."

"Hey, this is Griffin's friend, Mason," I began. "I just called to let you know that if you don't shut the hell up, leave Griffin alone, and stop being a disgusting cockroach, I'll call the cops on you and get your ass thrown in jail, got it? I will not let you talk to him this way. You may be his father, but you don't get to treat him like this. Remember what I said because I'm not joking around, and I'll be checking up on you," I told him and hung up. I looked over at Griffin who was crying. He looked up at me with tears streaming down his face.

"He's going to hurt you now," Griffin said, choking a little on his tears.

"Does he hurt you or Bridget?" I cringed.

Griffin shook his head. "Only me, thank goodness. I'd kill him if he touched Bridget."

"You're not going home tonight. You and Bridget are sleeping over," I ordered. "If he comes, I'll lock him out of the house and let the cops deal with him."

Griffin said nothing, and I sighed. I hated seeing him like this. In a way, Griffin was like a little brother to me, and I never wanted to see him hurt. I always tried to make sure he was okay, and if he wasn't, I'd destroy whoever caused it. I gave him a hug, trying to help the poor kid stop crying. Bridget and Lexi walked outside to the backyard right at that moment. When Bridget saw the scene, she ran over to Griffin. I let him go, so she could talk to him.

"You okay?" she asked her brother.

I handed Griffin's phone to her. I don't think she even finished reading them when she hurled the phone at the wall. That was expensive technology. She glanced at me, and I put a serious face on, trying to not interrupt her.

"I should be fine. We'll be leaving soon." Griffin gave her a sad smile and walked inside the house to be alone.

Bridget turned to me. "I hate that man."

Later that night, Ariel and Matt got home from packing up Matt's stuff, which wasn't all that much. He had one suitcase. It was as if he were only planning on staying here for a week. Bridget, Griffin, Lexi, and I were on the couch, watching TV. Matt walked out of Ariel's room and tapped me on the shoulder.

"Hey can we talk?" he asked.

I winced and got up. "Fine." I headed out to the front yard as Matt followed.

Once we got outside, I stopped on the porch, so we were in the light. "Well?" I questioned, giving him a face of utter judgment.

"I know you don't like me very much, and I seem like a weird guy who randomly popped into your family's life," he blabbed.

I stopped him there. "Ariel isn't a part of my family."

"Well, nonetheless, I just wanted to say that I understand. I don't expect you to like me. You don't have to if you don't want to, but I do hope we can get along someday," Matt expressed.

"Why?" I asked. "Why do you care?"

Matt looked toward the ground and exhaled, "Look. I'm going to ask you something, and I want you to answer honestly."

"I asked you a question first," I snapped.

"I know, but just humor me for a bit."

I sighed, "You're weird."

"Mason, have you ever felt like you didn't belong in this world?"

I laughed. Did he read my mind or something? "Why do you want to know?" I wondered.

"All right, I'll take that as a no." Matt headed back inside, but I stopped him.

"Wait. Yeah...I feel like that all the time," I told him.

Matt looked at me and smiled a bit. "You haven't changed."

I looked at him confused. "Excuse me?"

Matt started to head back inside, but I stormed after him, grabbing his arm. "What do you mean by you haven't changed? I've never met you before." I looked at him with uneasiness. What game was he playing?

"You'll understand eventually, Mason. Just be prepared. Your entire world is about to change." Matt looked me dead in the eyes.

I wanted to sock him right in the face. "You're crazy," I spat.

"Ariel!" Matt called out, looking at her direction.

She was sitting on the couch, reading a book.

"I'm leaving. I'll see you tomorrow," he told her and left.

I was about to follow him, but I decided to drop it and pound him the next day.

Days passed. Sadly, today was Saturday, and I was supposed to go camping. I've been getting to know Matt for the past couple of days. Getting to know him meant my willingness to talk to him. Every time I brought up the conversation of why he acted all weird when he said I haven't changed, he ignored me. He went on with his day nonchalantly, which angered me.

Even though I wanted to get information out of him, I still wasn't up for this, I hated camping. I hated sleeping on the ground. Why sleep on the ground when I could sleep in a nice comfortable bed? Matt drove all the way out to Turquoise Lake with us, and we set up camp within about an hour. I guess, in a way, I didn't mind being out in the woods. It was a nice getaway. Ariel wasn't here, which made it all the better.

"So, who wants to go fishing?" Matt asked us with a dorky smile.

"Okay," Lexi said.

"You two have fun. I'm staying here and building a fire," I told them.

Lexi sighed, "Mason, it's not even dark outside."

"So? I want to burn things." I smirked with my gaze fixated at the fire pit.

"Don't worry, Lexi. I'll make sure he doesn't burn the forest down." Griffin gave her a smile.

Lexi blushed slightly and bit her lip before walking toward the lake with Matt.

Something was going on with her. Why the hell did she blush? I went off into the forest to find firewood, and of course. Bridget and Griffin tagged along. It was pretty nice outside. The perfect amount of warm and cold. The only problem were the storm clouds, which meant it was probably going to rain. I picked up some sticks that looked suitable for burning. I didn't really know how to build a fire, but I was terrible at fishing and hated large bodies of water. The last place I wanted to be was by that lake though I studied it from afar.

I could see the water through a gap in between two trees. It was deep blue, not turquoise. Why they named it Turquoise Lake was beyond me. I didn't look long because I started to feel uneasy with all that water. I've had the fear of water ever since I almost drowned in the pool when I was little. That was a terrifying experience, and I haven't been in deep water since.

"Mason Gray... "

I panicked when I heard someone speak my name with my first name. I had no idea where the 'Gray' part came from. I looked around the perimeter but saw nothing. No one was anywhere near me except for Bridget and Griffin, but they weren't even close enough to whisper to me. I was still paranoid but slowly went back to picking up sticks.

"Mason, you must remember."

The voice came back, but this time, it was louder. I looked up again, but nothing was there.

"Hey, did you guys just hear something?" I asked Bridget and Griffin.

They both looked confused. "No...why?" Bridget asked.

I muttered, "Oh, nothing. Just my imagination...I guess."

Out of nowhere, I heard Lexi scream in the distance. My eyes peered toward the lake in panic and worry.

"Lexi?!" I yelled, dropping the sticks in my hands and booked it to the lake. Griffin and Bridget followed along.

Once we reached the lake, we saw something we thought we would never see. Lexi was all right, but she was running away from a wrestling match between Ariel and Matt. Ariel looked very different like a monster you'd see in horror movies mixed with Greek mythology. Her skin was all gray with light purple tattoos that looked like some form of ancient writing. Her hair was dark purple, and her face looked freaky as hell. She had the eyes of a snake, and her teeth looked razor sharp and very long. But the most frightening part was her eyes. They were white—just white, no pupil, no nothing. She had claws, and I was screaming inside at the sight.

I froze from fear; however, Griffin and Bridget ran toward the fight. Matt had a long sword in his hands. It had a black blade and rested on a gold hilt with a red ruby placed in the middle.

Griffin tackled Ariel to the ground, putting her into a head lock. But she managed to break out of his grip just enough to bite a chunk of his arm. Griffin screamed out in pain and let her go. Matt tried to stab Ariel who was now running toward me. He missed, and she tackled me to the ground. I screamed.

"You're lucky I have to keep you alive," she whispered to me as she forced me onto my feet to use me as a human shield. "Come any closer, and he dies," she told the others. Her voice changed to a deeper, more devilish voice.

Everyone went rigid. Matt still held up his sword, which was pointed it toward us.

"What the hell is going on?" I questioned with my voice shaking.

"Let him go," Matt ordered her with a powerful glare. "Qadir wouldn't want you to kill him. That's why he sent him here. So, he could stay out of the fight."

"You think I care? I will kill him unless you leave. Same with you two," Ariel said to them.

By that, I think she meant Griffin and Bridget. This was all so confusing. This couldn't be real.

"We will leave, but Mason and Lexi are coming with me," said Matt, keeping his glare on Ariel.

Ariel dug her nails into the neck. I let out a small cry of pain. I could feel blood slowly seeping from where she stabbed me with her claws.

"Leave him alone!" Bridget shouted and was about to storm at her when Griffin stopped her.

"We'll go, but they've seen you, Ariel. They will fight back. You wouldn't want that," Griffin said.

Ariel shot a sharp glance at him. "They don't even remember who they are," Ariel hissed.

"What do I not remember?" I was crying. I'm such a wimp.

Ariel snapped at me, "Shut it, you brat."

Bridget looked at Griffin with a worried look. He clutched his arm where he was bleeding badly.

Lexi walked over to Ariel and me, looking scared. Although she was shaking, she looked as if she were ready to kill. "Get away from my brother, you bitch." Lexi glared and threw her hand out in front of her body. A bright light shot from the palm. It was so bright that I had to close my eyes. Everything went quiet after a loud boom went by my ears.

Ariel had shot back, letting me go. Scorched and shriveled, she dropped onto the ground. *Poof!* And she turned into ashes.

"What the hell?!" I yelled, panicking.

"Mason, let me explain," Griffin said.

"Yes, please explain to me why my adoptive mother was a creepy monster and how my little sister was able to turn her into ash in a split second!" I shouted. My heart was racing. This had to be a dream.

"Mason, calm down," Bridget commented.

"Look, she wasn't really your adoptive mother. She only lived with you for a year. You actually aren't from this world," Griffin said calmly.

"Wait, is Mason still my brother?" Lexi asked.

"Yes," Bridget chuckled. "Qadir took over our world called The Realms or as some call it The Sacred Grove. He sent you both here because you're the only ones who can stop him."

"This is crazy," I said. "But seems awesome."

"Then why don't we remember that place, The Realms?" Lexi questioned.

"He erased your memories," Matt chimed in. "I'm your father. Well, I sort of adopted you."

"You're our adoptive father? Then who are our real parents?" I asked.

"Melanie, the goddess of life, and Alash, the god of death from The Sacred Grove. They are your parents," Matt said.

"Our parents are gods?!" I exclaimed. "This is so cool. Why didn't you guys tell me before?" I asked Griffin and Bridget.

"It wasn't the right time," Griffin said.

Bridget looked at his arm. "We should get you patched up."

"I'm fine. We need to get them caught up," Griffin told her.

"Let me just get this straight. Everything I know about this town is a lie?" I shuddered.

Matt nodded. "Yeah, you never grew up here."

I looked at Lexi. "And she has magic?"

Matt nodded again. "You both do."

"You have no idea how much I wanted this to come true, and now that it has, I'm so pumped." I beamed. Goodbye Leadville! Goodbye America! I'm out of here! Although I didn't know where I was going, I assumed I would remember once I got there.

"Wait, how do we get our memories back?" Lexi asked.

"I have Ambriel working on it. She should be able to restore your memories once we get back," Matt told us.

"Who's Ambriel?" My eyes widened.

"She's your guardian angel though not a very good one." Griffin smiled. "She'll be so excited to see you again, Mason."

I looked at Lexi with a big smile. "I have a guardian angel."

"Good for you," she chuckled.

"Okay, what are we waiting for? Let's go!" I shouted.

"Hold on. We have a lot more explaining to do. You need to get caught up just in case we can't restore your memories right away," Matt said. "So, let's start with this. I'm the king of the kingdom called the Sanctuary in the Summer Lands of the Sacred Grove."

"The Sacred Grove is so formal. Call it the Realms," Bridget said.

Matt went on, "Okay, the Realms. That's the world you were born in. Since I'm the king, you both are royals as well. Prince and Princess of the Sanctuary. However, the Realms has been taken over by Qadir, the God of Mischief."

"Oh, and the gods in the Realms prefer to be called sorcerers. They think *god* sounds too intimidating to the citizens of the Realms," Bridget added.

"Bridget, please stop interrupting. We need to hurry up and get this over with before Qadir sends anymore Twilight creatures," Matt told her.

"Right. Sorry." Embarrassed, Bridget grinned.

"What are Twilight creatures?" Lexi asked.

Matt looked at me for a second then turned to Lexi. "They are Qadir's army, who work for him. But they can be controlled by Mason."

"Wait. I could control Ariel? Why did no one tell me this before? My life would've been so much better," I remarked, sounding frustrated.

"Mason, shut up," Matt exhaled loudly. "You can control them because they're your creatures. You created them, but somehow, Qadir was able to take your power from you."

"So, I don't have magic?" I asked, feeling a little disappointed.

"Not right now, but you can get it back," Griffin said.

"Then let's go kick this guy's ass," I said.

"What part of *god* do you not get?" Lexi asked me with a snarky tone.

She had a point though. How would I beat up a god? I needed to think a little harder sometimes.

"Right now, Mason isn't a god. He used to be. But Lexi, you're a goddess," Matt looked at both of us.

"Sweet." Lexi smiled.

I sighed and looked around. All the excitement made me a bit tired. Also, all of this was a little mind-blowing. I just needed to step back into reality for a second. I stopped and looked at the pine forest of Leadville. So calm, so boring.

"Let's go. You can explain the rest in the Realms," I told Matt.

"How do we even get there?" Lexi always had to ask more questions.

Matt, Griffin, and Bridget all looked at the lake almost in sync. Griffin kind of screwed it up by sneezing right as they turned toward the lake. Otherwise, it would have been a perfect moment.

"The lake will take us back to the Sacred Grove."

My stomach went into a knot at the thought of having to go any closer to that huge body of liquid death. "Dang it," I muttered.

"So, do we just walk into the lake, and we're there?" Lexi asked.

"Yeah, pretty much. But you have to go all the way in," Griffin said.

"Okay, how do people not stumble into the Realms all the time?" I asked.

"You have to either possess magic or be with someone who does possess it," Griffin explained.

"Okay, let's go," Lexi said, taking my hand and starting to run toward the water.

I screamed and quickly pulled away. "No!" I yelled. "No!"

"Mason, seriously?" Lexi rolled her eyes.

"I hate water." I frowned. Suddenly, I was in the air. I realized Griffin had picked me up and was heading for the water. "How the hell are you strong enough to pick me up?!" I yelled.

"I'm a demigod, so I'm stronger than your average human," Griffin told me and kept going toward the water.

"I hate you!" I shouted as we reached the lake.

Bridget, Matt, and Lexi followed us. I closed my eyes and held my breath, trying not to panic as we went under.

CHAPTER THREE:

The Realms

Everything was spiraling, and bright lights flashed all around me. Just a few seconds later, I crashed onto the ground, and grass spattered in my face. I lifted myself up, spitting a few pieces out of my mouth. *Gross.* That's when I realized I was in the Realms. Shooting up onto my feet, I looked around at the amazing scenery, which was unlike anything I had ever seen. But to be fair, I didn't really get out much so I haven't seen a lot.

The trees were like skyscrapers. They towered over me so high that it hurt to look up to see how far they shot up into the sky. I didn't get to look at the scenery much longer because I heard a noise behind me. I quickly turned around and saw a girl. She was looking at me as if she were seeing a ghost. She was fair looking with reddish brown hair and a heart-shaped face. I couldn't take my eyes off of her. There was just something about her.

Tears began to well up in her eyes. "Is it really you?"

"You know me?" I questioned, stepping a bit closer to her.

"You mean you don't remember me?" Her voice began to choke. She had an English accent, which made her more appealing to me.

My heart felt like it was going to stop. I didn't know why, but I had a feeling she was important to me. "I can't remember anything about this world...I'm surprised it's even real," I chuckled a bit.

The girl swept the tears off her cheeks as they fell down her face. She sniffled a bit and nodded. "Oh, of course. He made you forget."

"I don't know who you are or what's really going on right now, but can I just say...you're very attractive," I told her, breaking the dramatic moment. But it was good because she blushed. That's good, right?

"You haven't changed one bit." She smiled, stepping up to me and pulling me into a hug. I hugged her back. Yep, my compliment must've worked.

She pulled away with a lingering smile on her face.

"I don't want to make this awkward, but what is your name?" I scratched my head.

"Caroline. You'll remember me soon," she said. "Come. I'll take you back to the camp."

Caroline... That name did ring a bell in my mind. "Camp?"

"Yes, the rebellion camp. Everyone will be so excited to see you again," She confirmed.

"Everyone?" I questioned.

Caroline giggled, "It's probably best you stop asking questions."

Grinning, I nodded and raised my hands in defeat. "Fair enough. Lead the way."

She took my hand and pulled me along with her as she went deeper into the woods. It wasn't long before we reached the rebellion camp. I wasn't really sure what they were rebelling against, but I had a feeling it was that Qadir guy Matt told me about...I think. The camp was bigger than I expected. I was expecting maybe one tent and a few people singing songs about the outdoors around a fire. Now that I think about it, that was kind of a stupid thought. Who lights a fire during the day?

The camp had a bunch of large, white tents everywhere, and people all over the place. I guess a lot of people really hated this Qadir guy. It was all so fascinating—so much cooler than Leadville. The camp was hidden beneath the vast canopy of the forest, causing the surroundings to be darker. It wasn't too dark but dark enough that the camp had to have torches lit in different places.

"This is so cool. I really wish I remembered this place." I smiled.

Caroline looked at me and smiled back. "You will soon. Ambriel thinks she found a way to restore your memories."

"Yeah, Matt said something about that," I told her as I continued to look around.

We walked toward one of the tents, and I could hear people arguing inside. As we entered, I saw a short woman giving an angry look toward Matt. She had long black hair that was tied back in a braid, her skin was tan, and she looked like she could be from China—though that probably wasn't possible because she didn't live on Earth. She wore a simple long sleeve shirt. It was black like her soul. I'm totally kidding…well, sort of. She definitely gave off that vibe. For a short person, she really was intimidating. The combat boots she wore added to I'll-kick-your-ass-in-a-heartbeat look, so she looked pretty tough. I wasn't really sure what they were arguing about, so I just watched them hoping I'd figure it out.

"We can't sit here forever, Susalea! I brought them back because they can save the Sacred Grove," Matt shouted.

So, her name was Susalea. Another name that rang a bell. I was in the right place for sure.

"You brought back an idiot and his kid sister!"

Susalea retorted. How was Matt not shaking in fear of this woman? When she said idiot, I figured she meant me since Lexi and I were the ones Matt had brought back.

"Susalea... Um, I found him," Caroline mumbled.

Susalea turned to her while eyeballing me. She walked over to us and looked me up and down with her arms crossed. "Welcome back, ya pansy," she said and punched my arm.

Holy balls, she was strong. I winced in pain when her fist made contact with my arm.

She chuckled, "Still a big baby, I see."

"I am not!" I shouted in defense.

Ignoring me, she turned to Caroline and gave her a hug. "I haven't seen you all day, how are you feeling?"

Caroline hugged her back. "I'm feeling so much better. After all, Mason is back," she said with a smile. "Though he doesn't remember anything," she looked at me as her countenance saddened.

Matt was standing by the desk, looking at a large paper. Curious as to what it was, I went over to him.

"Caroline, why don't you see if Ambriel has found anything yet on how to restore his memories?" Susalea said. "I have something I need to discuss with Mason."

Caroline nodded and headed out. Susalea turned to Matt and me, walked over, and sat in the chair by the desk. On the desk was a large map, a map of the

Realms or Sacred Grove, whichever you want to call this world. I'll just call it the Realms.

"You can go too, Matt. I just need to talk to Mason," Susalea remarked.

Matt sighed and left. I looked at Susalea, wondering what she could possibly want from me.

"So, it's been a year. You're eighteen now, aren't you?"

I nodded. "Yes."

"That means you're ready," Susalea said matter-of-factly.

That got my full attention. "Ready for what?"

"Qadir's plan. He already has the Realms, but he wants more," Susalea said.

"What else could he possibly want?" I asked. "How can he want more when he already has the world?"

"Well, there is you. He wants you desperately," she stated. "He's always been obsessed with you. Trust me. I know. I was forced to marry him, and all he'd do was think about you."

"You married the big bad Qadir?" I questioned, but my tone was more cheerful than I planned. She probably thought I found it funny that she was forced to marry a tyrant like him. I didn't find it funny, I swear.

"Yes, and Mason, you have to be careful. He's a very sick, twisted man. He also fancies men...especially you," Susalea told me. "His plan is to get rid of the sorcerers once and for all then take you and keep you as his own forever. This has been his plan ever since you were born. Something evil sparked in him once he saw you for the first time."

"But why?"

Susalea took a deep breath, "His motives and reasoning are unsure. However, I have a theory."

"Well, then tell me," I demanded.

"You were born with great power, but that power was that of darkness," Susalea began to explain.

I listened closely.

"You were the God of destruction, devastation, and evil. Your power could change a saint into a demon. You were created to lure people to you, so you could twist them into a demon. If they fell for it, they'd become a Twilight creature. A creature designed and formed to serve you and cause destruction."

Ariel was my minion? Sweet. "I don't understand. Did I somehow turn Qadir into a Twilight creature?" I asked.

"Yes, but being a god, he found a way to control himself. See, Mason, gods can be persuaded and turn to evil, but they are not easily controlled like mortals," Susalea said. "Look. Qadir was able to take your power from you. I'm not going to explain how because I don't know...only you do."

"Okay, so what plan am I ready for now that I am eighteen? Because you never really explained that," I said.

"Though he has taken your magic, its energy still thrives off of you. Now that you're eighteen, it's reached its maximum strength. He can now use the power of destruction to destroy every last Sonyin god in existence. If he does that, they can't take back the Realms," Susalea explained.

"I don't get it. Why haven't they taken it back already? Hasn't it been a year?" I asked.

"The gods don't like to get involved with political matters even if it's caused by one of them," Susalea informed me.

I sighed, "You have to be kidding me. This is their world. They take care of it, so why are they just letting him control the people?" I was ticked off. Did they really expect us to fight alone? And what did she mean by Qadir fancied me? I feel I should be worried. I needed to get my memories back, so I could go off and kick that Qadir's ass.

"It's complicated. But if the gods fight Qadir now, they will die. Unless Lexi, of course, fights with them," Susalea stated.

"Why Lexi? What does she do?" I asked.

"She's the goddess of light, basically the opposite of you. She can destroy the Twilight creatures and all of your power. It's the only way now." Susalea said, "However..."

"However?"

Susalea sighed and looked down. She was silent for a few seconds then looked back up at me. "You will die."

"What?!" I panicked. "To stop Qadir, I have to die!?"

"Yes, it feeds off of your energy. Lexi killing you is the only way," she confessed.

"Why her though? I don't want her to have to kill me! She's my sister, one of my best friends. It would break her." I continued to panic. "This can't happen. There has to be another way!"

"Mason, calm down. Do you want the entire camp to hear us? If they find out you have to die, they will stop fighting." Her face hardened.

I took a deep breath, "I just got here, and I find out I have to die. Why are you telling me this?"

Susalea sighed, "Because I know you'll do the right thing even if you're an idiot. I couldn't tell anyone else. Only you."

"So, you're asking me to die?" I squinted.

She nodded. "I'm sorry, but this world needs you to."

Taking another deep breath, I looked at my feet. "There's no other way?"

"Not that I can think of unless you can somehow get your powers back from Qadir. But I wouldn't suggest it...that power is evil. It corrupts and kills. It leaves no survivors, and you were never able to control it before. You're a good person. You would never intentionally turn someone into what you turned Qadir into. You did that by accident in a moment of fear," Susalea said.

"What happened? What was I afraid of?" I continued to ask questions. Poor Susalea probably felt as if she were taking a quiz on her knowledge of my life.

"I don't know, Mason. You never share your secrets with anyone but Bridget, Caroline, and Griffin," Susalea stated flatly.

"Why Caroline? Like I get Bridget and Griffin since I know them, but why her?"

"You trust her. After all, she is your girlfriend."

I smiled although the terrible news I just heard should've prevented me from that. I couldn't help it. I had a girlfriend, one as adorable as Caroline. "I scored."

"Yes, you do love Caroline a lot, which is good. After all, you could've had any girl in the Realms, but you chose her." Susalea smiled, probably happy the subject wasn't so grim anymore.

"I could have? Do I have another fan club? Because I had one in Leadville. They stalked me, and it was weird," I uttered.

"You always have, but your fan club in the Realms is much bigger than one at a high school. It's just one of the perks of being you. The power you were born with graced you with the ability to attract others to you. Over time, they even go crazy because of you. Qadir being an example," she explained.

"What's my past with Qadir?"

Before Susalea could answer that, Lexi entered. "Mason...it's all real," she said and walked over to me.

Smiling at her, I nodded. "Yeah, it's pretty great," I told her though it wasn't going to last long for me.

I knew I had to die. I couldn't just let everyone in this world die instead. The really hard part was that Lexi had to do it. She would never kill me. We love each other too much. We've always had each other's backs, and we promised we'd never leave each other behind. If I were to die, I'd have to trick Lexi into killing me. It was killing me already to think about this. Maybe if I continued thinking about everything Susalea just told me, I could die now, and we wouldn't have to worry about it.

"Your girlfriend is really nice, by the way." She winked. "She's a keeper."

"Yeah...right." I realized that right when I got a girlfriend, I had to die.

"You okay?"

"Yeah, I'm going to go find Griffin and Bridget," I muttered nervously and stormed out of the tent. What was I going to do?

I didn't bother with looking for Bridget and Griffin. I would've just gotten lost anyway. Instead, I went off on my own in the forest, taking a nice walk to think about everything. It wasn't even five minutes since I had returned to the Realms, and I was already being told I wasn't going to be around much longer. The only way to stay alive was to defeat Qadir. And if I took my powers back, it would simply make everything worse. More people would die than ever before. Why did it have to be so complicated? Why couldn't it be like a video game where all I'd have to do is save the world by listening to a fairy who tells me what to do all the time?

Frustrated, I kicked the ground. I guess I'm cool with dying. I mean as long as it's for the greater good. I resumed walking when I heard what sounded like a loud cry of an animal. I stopped and looked around, staying quiet to get what direction it was coming from. I headed in that direction, hesitating. I didn't even know what it was. As I got closer, the noise got louder, but it turned out to be a small black and white dog barking at the trees.

I stopped, confused. What was it barking at? I chuckled a bit because it was cute, "Hey puppy, over here," I said and walked closer to it. The puppy was too small to actually hurt me, so I wasn't afraid of it. It looked at me, and its tail started wagging frantically. It jumped up and hugged my leg the best it could, basically begging me to love it. I picked it up, and of course, I was smothered by a bunch wet dog kisses. I pet the dog, laughing. It was so cute. I loved it. "Stop it, you little punk. You're going to lick me to death," I continued laughing.

"He remembers you," someone said.

I quickly took my eyes off the dog and saw a man standing a few feet away from me. He looked pretty weird, wearing an orange tux with a blue tie, a somewhat-large orange top hat to match, and held a staff that looked like sapphire gemstones. His face looked tired, yet he was actually pretty good looking. But the outfit sort of killed any hope of him being attractive. He looked about thirty years old or maybe a bit older. His skin was an exotic tan, and his eyes were orange like sunset. It was odd, but I stopped questioning things like that when I saw Bridget's odd-colored, cyan blue eyes. His hair was pretty long and wavy too. It was a weird shade of blue that went down to his shoulders.

"Has he met me before?" I asked.

"Yes, he's your dog. Sparky is what you named him," the man said. His voice was gravelly. That went well with his masculine face, but again, not the outfit. I just didn't get the outfit.

"Sparky? Really? Okay, whatever," I said. "Who are you?"

The man smirked. "My name is Qadir. It's lovely to see you again, Mason.

CHAPTER FOUR:

Running

My heart stopped. This truly couldn't be happening. This was too sudden; I couldn't meet him just yet. I wasn't prepared or strong enough to fight him if it came down to it. Despite all that, Qadir was standing only a few feet in front of me. Knowing who he was made him seem frightening. But why was he here?

"You weren't supposed to return yet. You were supposed to stay in that small town where you were safe," he said.

"I...I hated it there," I mumbled.

Qadir snorted, "You're afraid."

Well, duh, of course, I was afraid. He just popped up out of the blue—the big bad villain of the Realms—

the tyrant God who seemed to destroy everyone and everything.

"It's all right. I understand," he said. "After all, the rebellion must've taken this opportunity to lie to you about me."

"Lie to me? They're my friends," I sneered, holding my dog Sparky close to me. I was ready to run whenever I needed to.

"Is that what they told you? Mason, they want you dead. They think you're a monster." Qadir told me. He had to be lying.

Matt was my adoptive father, right? Why would he be with the rebellion if they wanted me dead? Though he could be lying about adopting me, but what about Caroline? If Qadir was speaking the truth, was she a lie too? No, Qadir was the villain. I can't forget that.

"You stole my powers, you made me forget who I am, and you sent me to a town in an entirely different world. You let me live a lie and made me want to kill myself the entire time." I raged. "You're the one lying to me. I won't be fooled."

"I did that for your own good. I took your magic to protect you. It was driving you insane, changing you into something you are not. I sent you to that world so no one could hurt you. I even let your sister go with you, so you wouldn't be alone," Qadir said. He wasn't going to drop the act of appearing to actually care about me.

"Shut up," I said, glaring at him coldly.

"Mas—"

"No! Get out of here. I don't trust you," I shouted.

Qadir went silent and peered down at his feet, letting out a long sigh, "I was really hoping this would go differently."

"What makes you think it would have? From what I've seen you're the one hurting everybody," I said sharply.

"I was going to give you your memories back, but now, I won't," Qadir said as he approached me.

I quickly stepped away, but that didn't stop him. He just got closer and closer until I was backed into a tree. I guarded Sparky, so he couldn't hurt him. The last thing I wanted was an innocent dog being killed by this bastard.

Qadir got right up in my face and smirked. "I need to keep you alive. Now that you know why and how you'll die, I need to keep you far from it."

"So, they weren't lying? I knew it," I breathed.

"Don't you get it? I'm kidnapping you," Qadir announced with a smirk still planted on his face.

"Oh, are you now?" I questioned, and my heart began to race.

I had to find a way out of here quickly. I looked around… Nothing. I took a deep breath. I was going to have to drop Sparky, push him back, and make a run for it. I hoped that Sparky would follow, and hopefully dropping him wouldn't hurt him. He was a small Shih Tzu, so I didn't know from what height he could be dropped without getting damaged. But what else could I do? I couldn't let Qadir get me. I was the only way to stop him and the only way for him to succeed. Carefully, I attempted to set Sparky down, but Qadir quickly forced me back. He pinned me against the tree and slammed my head into the tree trunk. Luckily, I dropped Sparky as I planned. Pain filled my head, and I got dizzy, but now was the only chance. Sparky began to bark ferociously.

Qadir looked down at him. "I should've killed it a year ago."

He held his hand out just a foot over Sparky's head. His hand began to glow. I feared what would happen next. He was going to kill Sparky. I swiftly pushed him back before the beam of light could hit my dog. The light shot out of his palm as he fell back to the ground, hitting me instead. I dropped to my knees as Qadir shot up. Sparky continued to bark, and I was still on the ground in unbearable pain. It felt as if I were going to die, but Susalea said that the only person who could kill me was Lexi, so I wasn't concerned. Qadir stood above me, smirking at me in pain.

"Shall we get going then?" he questioned.

That's when I thought I was doomed. Sparky darted off into the woods. *Thanks for leaving me, buddy.* It was probably for the best. Who knows what Qadir would do to him? Qadir picked me up bridal style. *How embarrassing.* He was stronger than he looked. He was a tall yet scrawny man, so I didn't expect him to be able to lift me up as he did. He carried me deeper into the woods, but I was still in too much pain to fight back. I felt so pathetic. I couldn't fight him off, and the world was going to suffer for it. Eventually, we reached a large stone about the size of a horse that was floating in midair. It was white, glowing electric blue light that flowed inside the indents of the stone.

"What is that?" I asked sheepishly.

"A warp stone. It can take you anywhere in the Sacred Grove, and all you have to do is think about it. There's one in each kingdom," Qadir told me.

Looking up at the sky, I noticed something flying toward us. It appeared to be three giant eagles flying toward us. Qadir was about to touch the warp stone when a rock hit his head with a loud thud, causing him to drop me. After crashing to the ground, it took me awhile to fully comprehend what was going on. The eagles were flying all around Qadir, and they were huge.

Something was attached to the saddles on their backs, green booger looking trolls. They were attacking Qadir, backing him far from me and the warp stone. They were biting, slashing clawing, and dodging. However, Qadir could kill them all once he got a chance. Surely, they were brave little trolls. They had swords and wore clothes that humans would wear, which were covered in dirt and grime. They were gross looking, but thanks to them, I wasn't in Qadir's hands anymore. Immediately, I tried to get on my feet as they fought Qadir. He was angry beyond comparison. I could see the rage written all over his face. Qadir was throwing fireballs everywhere and whatever else he could conjure up.

Trying to stand, I grabbed onto the nearest tree and hoisted myself up the best I could. Luckily, Qadir's magic was wearing off. Abruptly, one of the trolls flew on its eagle over to me.

"You must get out of here quickly," it said, sounding tired and a bit in panic.

"Where do I go?" I asked, taking a quick peek behind him to see how the others were doing against Qadir. It didn't look good. One of the trolls—the one wearing a blue hoodie and swinging an axe around—was forced to fight Qadir on foot because his eagle was down. The other that wore glasses and what appeared to be a sweater vest was still on its eagle.

"Just touch the stone, and think seaside," the troll in front of me said. The troll had crazy eyes and wore punk-rock-looking clothes. Trolls in this world were weird.

"Will it work? I don't even know what seaside looks like," I muttered.

"Quickly. My buds and I will meet up with you later. You'll be find that all you need is a name or an image," the punker troll spoke fast.

"What about you guys?" I was a little worried for my rescue party.

"We'll meet you there. Go!" he yelled and went back to the battle.

Instantly, I backed up a bit as he flew back over to Qadir and watched them again. Taking a deep breath, I turned around and faced the stone. *God please say this works.* I put my hand on it gently and thought the word seaside.

Everything went dark for a few seconds. Maybe even a minute. I couldn't tell. I slowly realized I was no longer in the middle of the forest. I was lying face first in warm sand. It felt nice until a large wave swooped over me, and I was soaked. I let out a tiny scream, bolted up, and booked it away from the ocean. Unfortunately, I ran right into a palm tree.

"Ow."

I heard a few giggles behind me. Turning around, I rubbed my face and checked my nose to see if I was bleeding. I was okay though my face hurt a lot. I was embarrassed in front of a bunch of people. There was a huge party going on, and all of them were staring at me, whispering to each other. I was just standing there awkwardly until someone finally walked up to me and kneeled down on one knee. I began to panic inside. Were they proposing to me?! I took a step back.

He bowed his head to me. "Prince Mason, we have long awaited your return."

Oh, good. I don't have to reject a marriage proposal.

A woman walked up to us. They were both dressed in bathing suits because, obviously, it was a beach party. "Everyone in the Realms believed you were dead. This is a miracle." She smiled and bowed.

"I was compromised," I said, feeling nervous. Everyone was staring intensely at me.

A man stepped forward. He seemed angry and a bit frightened. "Do not bow to him! If Lord Qadir finds out that he's here, we are all dead," he said loudly so everyone could hear. "We have to turn him in."

"Qadir won't hurt any of you. I wouldn't allow that," I stated.

The man snorted, "You no longer have any power to stop him," he reminded me. "You're weak and useless. If you're the one who is supposed to save the Realms, then we are all dead men!"

"I don't need power to do what must be done," I said, standing tall. "Qadir will fall even if I have to die to stop him." I climbed onto a large rock that was only a few feet away, so everyone could see. I assumed I was important, considering they all seemed to know who I was. "Just because things are dark now doesn't mean they always will be. You have to be brave enough to see the next day, to see the sunrise! I promise you. I will stop Qadir. Don't lose faith like this man."

"Easy for you to say," a voice called out from the crowd. "You don't have Qadir's soldiers at your door, forcing you to give them everything you own. They aren't killing everyone you love. You're just hiding."

"I don't remember anything about my past right now, I'm kind of just going along with things. I don't know how you all feel right now, nor do I know if I have been through anything remotely close to what you're all facing. It must be hard to feel like there's no hope, to feel as if you can't do anything." I continued to preach, "But if I learned anything from last year, it's that no matter who you are, you can do the impossible. There is hope. You've just got to believe in yourself, and I ask that you believe in me."

"Prince Mason." The man who bowed to me earlier stepped up.

Now that I looked closely at him, I noticed that his nose was a bit crooked. I couldn't look away from it, and I felt bad, but it was distracting. He was wearing a grass skirt and looked Hawaiian. That's when I realized almost everyone here was Hawaiian. But I'm sure the Realms had different names for certain races. I wasn't going to strain myself over that because I never really cared about someone's race. Everyone was a person to me no matter what. Everyone here was wearing grass skirts, and some guys were even wearing coconut bras. The Seaside must be the Hawaii of the Realms.

"I am Chief Akamu, Leader of the Seaside. I'm servant of Asa who is the sorcerer of oceans and seas," he introduced himself. "We do not serve Qadir. He is not our ruler."

"That is good to hear, but be careful. I don't want him attacking your kingdom," I told him. It didn't seem like a kingdom, but it was too large of a land to be a town or village.

Chief Akamu smiled and signaled me to walk over to him. The entire crowd was still staring at us while music quietly played in the background. This place was definitely the party capital of the Realms. I could just tell. Jumping off the rock, landing in the sand, and grains flying up from the impact. I went over to him. "We will have a feast in your honor. The Guardian of the Realms has returned to save us again!"

Guardian? Okay, I could live with that.

"Wait. I want that guy locked up until I leave," I said and pointed to the man who spoke out against me. "In movies, guys like him always go off and tell the villain where the protagonist is."

"Sorry, Bill. You heard him." Chief Akamu gave Bill a quick look of disappointment.

I was disappointed in Bill too. A few guys with spears went over to Bill and dragged him toward a cave in the distance. I gave Bill a little wave as he glared at me, and I tried not to laugh. The amount of power I seemed to have over these people was probably not a good thing for me to hold, considering my maturity level wasn't very high for an eighteen-year-old.

"Let the celebrations begin!" Chief Akamu shouted, and the crowd cheered loudly, crowing and screaming with joy. Honestly, I wanted to cover my ears, but I was worried I'd offend them. I couldn't afford to upset an entire group of people. I had a feeling I was going to need as many allies as I could get.

CHAPTER FIVE:

Unfolding

An hour later, everyone was partying on the beach again. The feast was fun; however, I had no idea what most of the food was. The table was covered with different kinds of what I assumed were fruits. They looked and tasted like fruits though they were shaped weird. Some were blue and shaped like a raindrop, and inside was blood red with a texture somewhat like the inside of an apple but juicier. At first, it creeped me out because it looked like blood, yet it was fun to eat because you could pretend that you were eating the heart of your enemy.

Chief Akamu said that it was called the Thana Apple, meaning death apple. It grew in Blackwood— one of the thirteen kingdoms of the Realms—in the Autumn Lands. Most of the fruits that looked creepy inside came from there. I was told it was like a dark forest with a large castle in the middle of it. I wished I could see it because the way Chief Akamu described Blackwood. It seems really cool. The sky is always dark, there is literally never sun there, yet everything survives without a problem, which basically goes against everything I learned in science class...I love it.

The natives of Seaside were all vegetarians in honor of their god Asa. According to them, he was a vegetarian and refused to eat any kind of meat. I couldn't do that. I loved steak too much. I stayed far from the party on the beach. I wasn't really a fan of large groups of people especially ones that acted uncontrollably as if they were wild animals. There was a small village just north of the coast line, so I went there and spent my time at the cafe with Chief Akamu, whose name honestly made me laugh inside the more I thought about it. I really wished Bridget was here. She'd get a kick out of his name too. I was pretty lonely here. The only friend I had was the chief, but I barely knew him. And I didn't want to annoy him by following him everywhere.

I always worried about whether I was bothering someone or not. I may play it off as if I have a lot of confidence, and I typically do, but there are times— mostly when I am alone—that I get a little bit shy. My confidence level usually depends on if I'm around people I know and feel comfortable to be around. So, I was hiding at a corner table at the outdoor cafe they had by the village. People were laughing all around me. Tourists from other kingdoms were everywhere; some would even stop to look at me from a distance and whisper to their friends about me. My guess was that the news of my arrival got around fast, which couldn't be good because I didn't want Qadir to know I was here. In fact, I probably should start leaving, but I had no idea where to go.

"It really is you."

I looked up after I heard a voice of some girl walking up to me. I swore she was a goddess because she was breathtaking. She had gorgeous and long, curly blonde hair that went down to her butt. Her skin flawless yet oddly pale—however, it fit her very well. Her most eye-grabbing feature was her eyes, which were blood red. I couldn't look away once I saw them. I tried to speak to her, but I completely choked.

She giggled, "You're so cute," she said.

I stayed quiet and just smiled a bit. Why was I so embarrassing? She was wearing a bikini with tight shorts and white flip flops to match her bikini top. The girl sat down at the table with me with a smirk on her face.

"I missed you a lot, Mason."

"You know me?" I managed to ask without a problem.

She smiled and slid closer to me on the bench. "Everyone knows you, but we've been friends for years." She continued to get closer until there was no gap between us. "I'm Emilia. Does that ring a bell?"

I was feeling a bit awkward with her this close to me, I was a fan of keeping my own personal space. "Sorry, but no," I told her.

She pouted, biting her lip, and reached up to stroke my cheek with her hand.

"What are you doing?" I asked, backing up a bit. Her skin felt ice cold.

"You're so handsome," she said and leaned toward my face.

I got up on my feet. "Thanks. I'm just going to go now." I smiled nervously and walked off, hoping to find the way out of Seaside. I had to get back to Lexi, Bridget, Griffin, and the others.

"Mason, wait!" she called out, following me. "You need to get back to the rebellion, right? I can get you there."

I stopped and spun around. I almost ran into her because she was closer than I thought. "Who are you? Enemy or friend? No, wait. Don't answer that. I can't trust you."

"Yes, you can," she said.

"No, I can't trust anyone until I get my memory back," I told her.

"Mason, please, I promise you that I'm on your side," she pleaded.

I just turned back around and kept walking, heading farther away from the cafe and Emilia.

"Mason!"

"Leave me alone, please," I uttered while still walking. I didn't know why I suddenly got so dejected, but it finally hit me that I was home. I just couldn't remember anything of it. I felt like the Mason they all knew was another guy. This feeling would probably go away once I had my memory back, but for now, it would bug me endlessly. I had to get back to the people I had memory of—Lexi, Bridget, and Griffin.

Emilia grabbed me, and I immediately stopped. I looked at her stunned and angry. Her hand gripped my wrist tightly.

"Let go of me," I sneered and tried to break her grasp, but nothing happened. She was too strong.

"Don't bother struggling," she said.

I looked her right in the eyes with my coldest glare, but it didn't last long. When I looked at her, I noticed the veins under her eyes were huge, and her irises had turned black. She looked like a demon, and it didn't help that her canine teeth were fangs. She looked like one of those vampires in the teen vampire romance shows that Bridget always made me watch.

Before I knew it, she threw her head back while forcing me to reveal my neck. As she sunk her fangs deep into my flesh, I screamed in pain. I could literally feel her draining me of my blood. I was getting weaker as each second passed. You think that the vampire movies would teach you how to break out of a vampire's grip, but they didn't. Now, I was screwed. Emilia let me go and gasped as I fell to the ground. I was so dizzy. Lying there almost lifeless, I saw Susalea, Bridget, and Griffin running over to us. Emilia appeared next to me on the ground…unconscious. She had a dagger in her back.

"What did you hit her with?" Griffin asked Susalea once they reached us.

"The dagger was laced with roses," Susalea said.

"That can hurt a vampire?" Bridget questioned.

"Yes, roses have the effect on vampires that garlic would have if that was actually a thing," Susalea explained.

Griffin kneeled beside me, checking to see if I was still alive. "He's breathing, but barely. Where's Ambriel?" Griffin asked, looking at his sister.

"She went to warn the people to get out of here. The Twilight creatures will be here any minute," Bridget panted.

"I have to go to the medical clinic to see if I can find anything that can heal him up quickly. Griffin, stay here with Mason. Whatever you do, don't let the Twilight creatures touch him. Now that he's back in the Realms, they can turn to him as a life source, and that wouldn't be good because they'd be stronger than they already are," Susalea told Griffin.

"How much stronger?"

"Strong enough to not be able to die from a mortal blade or any blade for that matter other than celestial blades," Susalea said, pulling out a small knife.

"You're going to kill Twilight creatures with that?" Griffin asked, but Susalea just ignored him and ran off.

"You'd figure Emilia would have given up on Mason by now," Bridget commented. She looked at me. "Is he awake?"

Griffin nodded. "Yeah, He may be mortal now, but he's still stronger than the average human."

"Come on, Mason. Get up. These people need our help, and they might not make it out in time," Bridget said as she kneeled beside Griffin and me. She was right. I needed to get up. My senses were fine, but I just felt so drained. If I stayed here, I wouldn't be able to save anyone from the Twilight creatures' attack on Seaside.

"Do you think Asa will come to the kingdom's aid?" Bridget asked Griffin.

"The sorcerers have been silent for over a year now, so I'm not even sure they're still alive," Griffin told her.

"Someone should go to Kule and check on them," Bridget said.

"There's a problem with that. No one knows where Kule is. And besides the gods, the only people who would know can't remember anything," Griffin sassed. He was obviously a bit on edge; otherwise, he wouldn't normally sass his sister like that.

Bridget slightly panicked at Griffin. "He doesn't remember how to fight."

"He won't be fighting anyway. Not like this." Griffin turned to Emilia who was still out cold. "What do we do with her?"

"Leave her. Let the Twilight creatures get her," Bridget said, pulling out a water bottle from her bag. She began to open the lid.

"What are you doing?"

"I'm going to pour water on him and see what happens."

"I doubt that would work," Griffin sighed.

"Like you said, he doesn't function like normal humans," Bridget pointed out. "It could work."

"He's not even unconscious. Just wait for Susal—" Griffin immediately shut up when he heard a loud boom and screams coming from the village. Both of them looked toward the noise in shock.

"They're here," Griffin said with a frightened tone.

"Let's get him off the beach," Bridget suggested, and they tried to help me up. They were able to get me on my feet.

"You feel any better, Mason?"

"No..." I managed to speak though my voice was quiet.

"Let's hurry," Griffin said.

We headed toward a couple of palm trees that were grouped together and surrounded by tropical-looking bushes. Once we got there, Griffin let me go and moved, so some of the bushes could hide us. That's when I went crashing to the ground because Bridget got distracted, letting me fall.

"Bridget, really?" Griffin seethed.

My head hurt like hell now.

"Sorry," Bridget whispered.

That's when I decided to try to get up despite how terrible I felt. The screams never stopped. The terror in the air was tangible. Griffin and Bridget watched everything closely, but I couldn't see anything. The looks on their faces gave me the impression that I didn't want to know what those creatures were doing.

"Oh, gods, Griffin. They're coming this way," Bridget whispered to her brother in panic.

"I'll distract them. You get Mason out of here," Griffin told her.

"I'm not leaving you behind." Bridget shook her head.

"Go now," Griffin ordered.

I got up, stumbling slightly, but I was able to stand on my feet. That was progress.

"Mason," Bridget uttered and looked at me. "Tell Griffin he is being stupid and that we need to stick together."

Ignoring Bridget, I looked toward the Twilight creatures, and they were heading right for us at a fast speed. They looked different than Ariel and were almost like shadows with bright red eyes. Some features were the same as Ariel's such as the tattoos all over their bodies, but they were a bright glowing red. They looked less human and more frightening.

"What happens if they touch me?"

"You're forced to take your magic back. You may not remember, but when you had your powers, you kind of got very depressed. So, I suggest we avoid the Twilight," Griffin explained.

"Good. Then we fight," I said, staring at the creatures, feeling a bit frightened but mostly angry.

The village burned behind them with rage, and the screams slowly faded. What was most scary to me was that I knew when someone had died. Every death that was caused by the Twilight gave me strength. Every time someone died, I grew stronger, and the Twilight grew stronger too.

"Did you even listen to what I said?" Griffin asked. He seemed offended that I've ignored his words. I believed we could fight. I just couldn't get close to them.

"Do you even remember how to fight?" Bridget asked.

I shook my head but still stood there as heroically as I could without looking like a cocky bastard. "Not a clue, but I have a feeling I'm going to regret ditching gym class."

"He can't fight those. I won't let him take control of the Twilight again," Griffin argued.

Bridget chuckled and held a ring out to me. "I've been keeping this safe ever since you left."

I gazed down at the ring, which was silver with black engraving on the sides that said something in what looked like elvish, but I couldn't make it out. In the center, there was a blue gemstone in the shape of an eye.

"It's your guardian armor. Just press the gemstone like you would with a button. Before you know it, you'll be ready for battle."

"That's so cool." I smiled.

Quickly taking the ring from her, I put it on and pressed on the gemstone. Suddenly, a bright light shot from it, spinning all around me. Before I knew it, I was wearing a navy blue jumpsuit with a silver belt that was very fitting on me. Most jumpsuits I've seen were pretty baggy, but this one was perfect. I could tell it would be easy to run around in it. On my back was a silver symbol of a tree stitched onto my torso. I saw it in the reflection of the waterfall behind us. My favorite part was the weapon that was a titanium bow with a dark blue trimming. I had a feeling that blue had always been my favorite color. A quiver matching my bow was on my back with full of black arrows.

Luckily, the Twilight creatures were inspecting every inch of the beach though we were pretty far away from them, thank goodness. Taking a deep breath, I readied my bow, putting an arrow in place, and aimed for one of the creatures. I was hoping that I was actually good at this.

"Shoot it now," Bridget said. "I want to watch that bastard die."

When I released the arrow, it whistled through the air, hitting a creature straight in the head. It dropped to the ground and vanished, leaving only my arrow behind. "Did it die?" I asked, curiously looking at my friends.

Griffin smirked. "Yeah, you got it."

That's when I realized that they had changed into the same jumpsuit uniforms as I had on, except Bridget's was dark purple, and Griffin's was green. It kind of reminded me of the power rangers, but we looked cooler than them, I swear.

"Then let's get this fight started!" I shouted, and we charged into battle.

CHAPTER SIX:

The Massacre

We had been fighting for a while, and I made sure to keep my distance from the Twilight creatures. Smoke floated all around us. The screams had left, but the sound of battle still roared in my ears. Surprisingly, I hadn't died yet nor gotten hurt. I've been sitting on a boulder, shooting Twilight creatures left and right. Griffin and Bridget seemed to be holding up pretty well, but they seemed a bit tired now. Who wouldn't be tired from fighting all these things? And it was only the three of us. We were doing pretty well, but eventually, they'd overrun us since there were so many of them. I wanted so badly to save the people of Seaside that I just jumped into battle without thinking.

"We have to get out of here!!" I yelled. "Go. I'll hold them off!"

"We aren't leaving you!" Griffin shouted as he cut the head off of a Twilight creature with his sword. I was really impressed with how he fought. He was the best swordsman I had ever seen. Bridget fought with a scythe, and she was very skilled with it. She could kill over five Twilight creatures in one swing. She was so cool.

"I said go!" I ordered them.

Griffin hesitated, deciding to book it to the village.

"Be safe!" Bridget ran after Griffin when she got the chance.

The twilight creatures were about to chase them when I shot them dead.

"Hey! Up here! Come and get me," I said, desperately trying to get their attention.

They shot their gaze toward me and charged. I got my arrows ready. This was the moment. I realized I needed to think things through. How was I going to take on all these creatures alone without getting touched? I let my arrow fly straight into the eyeball of the closest Twilight creature, and it dropped dead. I had to find a way out of this mess.

"Okay, this is not fair! There are so many of yo—" before I could finish yelling, I was lifted into the air. "Whoa!"

"Don't worry Mason. Your princess is here to save you," Caroline said from above.

I looked up, and there she was, riding on the back of a dragon. My girlfriend was a boss. She was smiling down at me as the dragon took us away from the Twilight creatures. It clutched my body tightly, so I wouldn't slip out of its grip.

Smiling back, I gave her a little wave. "Thanks. I was screwed down there," I shouted.

"How many times am I going to have to save you?" she shouted back.

"Who knows?" I chuckled.

She giggled a bit then smirked, looking forward. "Where's Bridget and Griffin?"

"Last I saw them, they ran off into the village," I told her.

Then three giant eagles abruptly flew up next to us, and I knew who it was right away. The three trolls from before.

"Greetings, Prince Mason. How may we be of assistance?" The blue hooded troll said to me, saluting.

"Um, I don't know... Caroline?" I peeked up at her, hoping she had ideas.

"Find Bridget and Griffin for us, and I'll take Mason to Lexi. She and Ambriel are trying to find a way to extinguish all the fire," Caroline said.

"Will do," the troll said. Snot dripped out of his green, bulgy nose. It was nasty.

"Good luck, Zack." Caroline smiled, and the dragon swooped down, leaving the eagle-riding trolls to find my best friends.

So, the trolls actually had names? Zack was the name of the one in the blue hoodie. I wondered what the others' names were.

Before I knew it, I was with Lexi. She was standing on the beach with a girl who looked about my age. She wore a long and flowing, sleeveless, periwinkle dress that went down to her heels in the back and to her knees in the front. I knew girls had a name for that kind of dress; however, I had no clue what it was. Her skin tone was a beautiful olive, and she had her light brown hair up in a bun. She was stunning from a distance and was even more beautiful up close. Was everyone in the Realms naturally attractive? I assumed that she was Ambriel, and I was right. My guardian angel, who was supposedly bad at her job.

We landed, and I had claw marks on my side from the dragon holding me so tightly. That stupid purple piece of nothing did help save my life, so I forgave it. Once Lexi saw me, she ran, pulling me into a big hug.

"I was so worried," she told me as she hugged me.

That's when I realized we were surrounded by dead bodies. They just lay there motionless... It was horrifying. They were all so pale and lifeless. To think that not too long ago they were all still alive. I had been with them and promised that I would protect them, but I failed. I didn't even try. I couldn't help but hate myself at that moment. I immediately pulled away from my sister's grasp and just stared at the blood-stained beach that was scattered with dead bodies. How could someone do this?

That's when I saw him...Chief Akamu. My heart shattered. I couldn't breathe. He had so much faith in me; he was so kind to me. Choking up a bit, I felt a tear fall down my cheek.

"I know it's horrifying," Caroline said and took my hand. "We couldn't get them out of here in time."

"Did everyone die?" I asked, feeling emotional. It was embarrassing. Guys weren't supposed to cry. They were supposed to be tough, right? Nah, that's stupid. This was too painful. Why hold the emotion back? A word of advice to everyone. Cry if you need to. Screw what anyone else says.

Caroline nodded. "I'm sorry."

"If we don't get out of here, we'll all die too," stated the girl who I assumed was Ambriel.

"Well, that's obvious," Lexi sassed.

I kneeled down next to Chief Akamu. I only knew him for a little while, and who knows maybe I knew him longer, but he was my friend. He had faith in me. He thought I was going to free his people, and look what I did. I was still crying.

Caroline kneeled beside me, wrapping her arms around me and putting her head on my shoulder. "Do you want to give him a funeral?" she asked somberly.

"We don't have time for a funeral. The Twilight is probably heading for us right now," Lexi said.

"Can't we hold them off just a bit longer?" Caroline asked.

"We can take him with us," Ambriel declared. "Caroline, your dragon can carry him," she said. She thrust her hands to her sides, and giant snow white wings shot out of her back. A few feathers detached and gently floated through the air. "Let's go."

"What about Griffin, Bridget, Susalea and the troll brothers?" Lexi asked.

"We'll just have to trust that the gods will bring them out of this safely," Caroline said.

"What have the gods ever done for us?" Ambriel remarked.

You'd think an angel would have complete faith in their gods, but I guess that wasn't the case for Ambriel.

"The only gods that have ever done anything for me are Mason and Lexi, but they aren't even acknowledged as real gods they truly are. It's bull crap."

She was a very odd angel.

We heard screeches of deranged beasts coming toward us. As much as we didn't want to, we had to get out of here. Caroline and I hopped onto the back of her pet dragon, and she informed me that his name was Jiggles and that I had given him to her. So, my escape car was Jiggles the purple dragon. Lexi and Ambriel followed us as we flew off—Ambriel, using her wings and Lexi, on a very large swan. It all freaked me out a bit. How were animals so big in this world? Were all animals over-sized? If I went for a walk in the forest one day, would I stumble across a giant bunny eating a tree like it would a carrot? Once I got my memory back, this would all make sense, and I wouldn't be so confused. I wouldn't be so useless... hopefully.

Jiggles carried Chief Akamu's body with us as we flew over the great sand dunes that separated the Seaside's tropical environment and the summer-like forest setting in the next kingdom. About ninety percent of the Realms was forest with the ten percent being Seaside. To me, it was perfect. I loved large forests especially ones with really tall trees that had deep green leaves that grew almost like a roof over the forest floor where it only allows just enough sun to keep things growing. That's why I loved the Realms. Everywhere was like that. Just endless forests with hidden wonders. Why would anyone want to destroy this? Why would Qadir want to ruin such an amazing world?

"Where are we going?" I eventually asked after I stopped zoning out.

Caroline glanced back at me. "Epona in the Spring Lands. We can give him a proper funeral there."

"I don't want to go anywhere I can get more people hurt," I told her. Looking back toward the

Seaside, I saw smoke rise from the village. We were pretty far from it now, but I could still see it.

"Don't worry. As long as we keep a low profile, no one will get hurt," she assured me.

I only nodded, still staring at the disaster behind me and hoping Bridget, Griffin, and the others got out safely.

CHAPTER SEVEN:

Memories

It was a few hours before we reached Epona. It looked similar to the forest the rebellion was in, which was probably normal for the Realms. We landed by a lake, and I grew very uneasy. I needed to get over my fear of water. After all, what kind of hero is scared of water? I had heard that in order to not be afraid of something anymore, you need to find out what caused the fear to begin with and overcome that. Unfortunately, I had no idea why I was so afraid of water. I always just assumed I feared drowning, but who knows? Maybe when I get my memories back, everything would be explained.

The funeral for Chief Akamu was small, short, and simple. We found a spare rowboat that was probably owned by some fisherman who left it there and now will never get it back. We placed flowers all around his body and said a few words before we set him drifting off into the water. Lexi has lit it on fire, and we watched. Since Lexi had her memories back, she knew how to use magic. I was jealous. Even if I had my memories, I no longer had magic. I was just awesome with a bow or best in the land. At least, that's what Caroline claimed. I asked her a lot about my life before I went to Leadville. I had been dating her for two years apparently. I had a lot of enemies—mostly jealous guys whose girlfriends I stole from them. I can't fathom why I would do that. Caroline says that I didn't intentionally steal their girlfriends. The girls just were a part of my fan club. I have a fan club here too, which I don't get because I'm not that great. Since they were a part of my fan club, their boyfriends blamed me for getting dumped, and there was a group out there who works for Qadir called the Pretty Boy Crushers, which consists of boys who want me dead.

It's really stupid. I know. I laughed a lot when Caroline told me about them. According to her, the president is named Brad Hart whose story is a little different than the other members of the Pretty Boy Crushers. Brad was a knight of the Sanctuary, the kingdom I lived in before I was forced to live in Leadville. Matt was the king, who was my adoptive father, so that made me Prince of the Sanctuary, and I got to boss Brad around. Well, one day he and Bridget started dating. I guess I didn't approve, so Griffin and I figured out a plan on how to break them up. It worked, and Bridget dumped him, but it somehow resulted in Brad thinking Bridget and I were secretly dating, so he thought we all were just screwing with his feelings. That's when he quit being a knight and founded the

Pretty Boy Crushers. When Caroline told me that story, I just couldn't believe it—still can't, but we will see.

Suddenly, we heard a loud caw of an eagle, and the rest of the group came flying down toward us on Eagles. I ran to my best friends and hugged them. Bridget hugged me back—she gives the best hugs. Griffin wasn't a hugger, so I let him go when he started to pull away.

"I was worried you guys were dead too," I said in relief and let Bridget go.

"Griffin!" Lexi yelled and ran toward Griffin. Once she reached him, she pulled him into a kiss, and my mouth dropped.

"What the balls?!" I shouted in horror.

Bridget laughed.

Griffin pulled away from Lexi and looked at me. "Oh, right. You don't remember. Lexi and I have been dating for a while now. She forgot, but she remembers now."

"You're dating my sister?!" I yelled in rage. I honestly was about to attack him, but Bridget stopped me.

Griffin stepped back a bit. "I'm sorry."

"This is why we never told you, Mason. Gods stop treating me like a child and jut accept that I love him," Lexi sassed me.

"You want to go?! I am allowed to be mad right now!" I shouted.

"Mason, shut up. Someone could hear us." Susalea rolled her eyes as she walked past us with the trolls.

"Ambriel and I will go set up camp" Caroline and Ambriel walked off into the forest.

"Stop controlling me!" Lexi then shouted.

"I'm not! I'm pissed my best friend and my little sister are dating, and no one told me! You didn't even tell me before we went to Leadville?!" I ranted.

"I didn't because I knew you'd act like this." Lexi rolled her eyes at me. "Matt even took this better than you."

"So, you told Matt but not me?"

"Can you two stop bickering already? I'll be at the camp." Susalea headed in the direction of Caroline and Ambriel, and the trolls followed her as they wrestled with each other a bit.

I sighed, "Forget it. You could have worse boyfriends."

"I did have a worse boyfriend. His name was Alex. He cheated on me, but don't worry. You and Matt destroyed him." She smiled.

"Sorry, Mason, I didn't mean to make you mad." Griffin pouted.

"It's okay, Griffin. Let's just go with the others to camp," I said and headed into the forest.

Bridget followed. Griffin and Lexi stayed behind, and I honestly didn't want to know why.

As we walked, I looked at Bridget. "Please tell me you don't have any secret boyfriends I don't know about."

Bridget chuckled, "I'm single for now."

Once we got into camp, I went up to Caroline who was talking to those trolls, Zack, and whatever the others were named.

"Hi, Mason." Caroline smiled.

Ambriel and Susalea were getting a fire started since the sun was setting—no tents in case we needed to leave quickly.

"Prince, Mason." Zack the troll bowed and put his hand on his heart, or at least, I think that's where his heart is located. I wasn't a master of troll anatomy. "I am Zack, one of the troll warriors who have dedicated their lives to the Sonyin Sorcerers."

The punk troll stepped up and did the same. "I am Phillip, the assassin troll of the troll warriors," he said and stood up, looking at me. "I, one day, want to be an assassin for the royal family of the Sanctuary... your family."

"And I, a knight," Zack commented.

"I'm Jordane," the third troll in the sweater vest said, fixing his glasses. "And I want nothing but to actually survive this war unlike these idiots who plan to die."

"As you can see, Jordane is the lame one," Zack remarked.

"Hey!" Jordane shouted in offense. His voice was shrill and a bit high pitched. In fact, they all sounded like prepubescent teenage boys.

Phillip laughed, which sounded a bit creepy like a demon in the night awaiting your murder mixed with a demented clown or something like that. "Nerd," he said and punched Jordane in the arm.

Jordane tackled Phillip, and they started wrestling.

"Men, this is not how you behave in front of royalty!" Zack shouted and went after them as they rolled away.

I then looked over at Caroline and chuckled, "They are something. Have I known them for long?"

"You knew them for a few weeks, then Qadir took you away," Caroline said. "It's been a lonely, depressing year without you."

"What happened? How did he send me away?" I questioned.

Caroline began to walk off. Naturally, I followed. "It was just you, me, and Lexi," she began. "You had your powers then. He took them before he sent you away…you were in so much pain when he did. It was like he was ripping your soul out. It was frightening. I tried to help, but he had some soldiers of his hold me back, and Lexi was unconscious. He erased her memory first."

"Why didn't he take her powers?" I asked.

"Something involving him exploding if he did. Light and dark are polar opposites. The only ones who could contain both of them is you and Lexi," Caroline stated. "In fact, that's what he wanted you to do to Lexi, take her magic so you were literally all the light and darkness of the world. You refused."

"So, he got rid of us? Why?" I questioned though Caroline probably didn't know everything. "I want this all to make sense. You have no idea how confused I am. It's killing me not to know anything. I feel so stupid."

She took my face in her hands and looked me right in the eyes. "Mason, it's okay. It's not your fault," she said while not breaking eye contact.

I couldn't look away either. She was so beautiful. At least, there was something I knew. I knew her. I knew how much I loved her.

"I would explain more, but honestly, you look exhausted. Let's go get some sleep."

"Okay." I gave her a small smile and took her hand, holding it tightly and heading back to camp.

I woke up in a small dark space. The ground was damp, and soil like dirt was all around me. I sat up looking around, and it was so dark. The air was thin and cold. I was shivering. That's when a light appeared above me. I turned my gaze up. I was in in a deep hole in the ground. A man stood above me. His face was unfamiliar, but he looked almost like an older version of me. He wore a black suit that was all I could see. It was hard to tell from so far away. Laughter began to echo all around me that was his laughter. That's when I realized I could see around me. I looked down and was petrified. Blood was all over me, and I was sitting in a pool of it. It was all over my shirt, my pants, my hands, and even my face. I just looked at my hands in horror.

"My son, look at what you have done...such a monster," the man snickered.

I began to panic, not knowing that it was about to get worse. Right in front of me was a cold, dead body, the body of my little sister, Lexi. She was pale white, ice cold, and stained with blood. It was such a horrific sight that I let out a scream, "You should have died! You should have never been born!"

The man continued to torment me. "She'd be alive if it weren't for you."

Shooting up suddenly, I realized it was all just a dream, but it scared me more than anything. What was that? Caroline was fast asleep on the ground beside me. She looked so peaceful, and just seeing her calmed me down a bit. I felt safe with her. I stood up carefully, trying not to wake up Caroline. Maybe a walk would make me feel less shaken up.

It wasn't long until I was far from the camp. I left little marks in some of the trees that only I could see just in case I got lost. Was that man in my dream my father? My real father? Could I be remembering things? No...that couldn't be a memory or even close to one. I refuse to let it be. I loved my sister. I would never kill her or hurt her. Or at least, I don't think I would...

It was all too quiet. I needed something to distract me. So many thoughts were running through my head that I wanted them to stop. But usually, getting thoughts out of my head was hard. I dwelled on them and never seemed to be able to let them go. It was times like this that the voice in my head got louder, and ignoring them was harder. The voices were always against me too. Always telling me how worthless I am and that I'm horrible and useless. At times, I believed them.

"Mason..." A voice said behind me.

I spun around and saw Lexi standing a few feet away. "Lexi? Did you follow me all the way out here?"

"Obviously. Otherwise, I wouldn't be here," Lexi said. "I was awake and saw you leave. Are you okay?"

It was a bit of relief to see her alive. After that dream, I needed a reminder that I didn't actually kill her.

"Yeah, I'm fine. Just trying to figure some stuff out," I told her. "Everything has been happening so quickly. There's so much to wrap my head around."

"Ambriel can make you remember as she did me," Lexi stated. She stepped a little closer to me, so she wasn't so far away—a less formal distance. "Though...I honestly don't think you should."

"What do you mean?" I asked. "Why shouldn't I?"

"It's hard to explain, but before you lost your memory, you were kind of off," Lexi confessed. "You always ignored everyone but your friends. You even ignored Cano, Max, Matt, and me, and you were so—"

I stopped her there. "Who's Max and Cano?"

"Our adoptive brother and technically stepmother. Cano is a witch, but she's still family though. Max is a cutie pie. He looks like a little version of Matt. He's super sweet but..." Lexi drifted, leaving her sentence unfinished.

"But what?" I asked. Why did she always have to be so dramatic? Just finish the sentence Lexi, and stop leaving me wondering.

"Qadir has him," she said. "He's been gone for a while. About a year and half."

"We have to find him," I declared. "Now, if he's family, we can't leave him behind."

"Mason, he's probably already dead," Lexi spoke sadly.

"You can't just drop a bomb on me like that!" I shouted. "Seriously, Lexi? I want my memories back. I'm sorry I ignored you, but that will change now for sure. I will still be the way I am now. I promise," I told her, hoping to reassure her that I always had her back. She was my sister.

"Okay," Lexi said and put her hand on my head.

"What are you doing?" I questioned.

"Giving you your memories back," she told me.

"You can do that?" I continued to question her, but I needed to stop asking questions.

"Just shut up for once in your life," she snapped.

"Don't tell me to shut up," I snapped back.

Lexi whacked me on the head at that second. "You're such a tart."

"Ow! Did you really just call me a tart?" I glared and rubbed the side of my head. *Damn. She hits hard.*

"Stand still and don't say anything," she ordered me and put her hand on my head again.

"Please don't kill me," I commented.

She just rolled her eyes and concentrated. I closed my eyes. The last thing I wanted was to watch my head explode. After all, she was the only person who could actually kill me. Out of nowhere, her hand suddenly felt burning hot, and a bright light flashed. That's when images of my past began to flood my mind. It was working. I saw my entire life flash before my eyes literally. It was all so much to take at once, but the closer we got to the present, the slower the images went. There's so much about my life that I never thought was possi— Oh, no.

CHAPTER EIGHT:

Distressed

What have I done? Everything with Qadir, the Twilight, and even Leadville was because of me. It was so hard to believe, but now I knew everything. What made it worse was that I planned to return from Leadville and finish what I started. I needed to disappear for a while. People were getting suspicious. Qadir didn't force me away. I left willingly, and I took Lexi with me so that she couldn't find out about what I was really planning. What was I planning? Murder, the destruction of an entire world. I truly frightened myself now... I even planned the attack on Seaside. I planned it all; everything was mapped out in my head. Qadir didn't send the Twilight there because I was there. All of those people would've died anyway.

This war, the lives lost...were all a part of my little game. A game I no longer wanted to be a part of. What was I going to do? I was in too deep; I was the head of the operation. Qadir and the Twilight were just my pawns. I had the entire world fooled. They all thought I was some hero, but I was the exact opposite. I was a monster.

"Did it work?" Lexi asked, and I stumbled away from her a bit. She gave me a worried look. "Mason?"

"Uh...yeah, I remember. It's all good." I smiled. "This is great. I am no longer confused." I didn't want to tell her. How could I tell her? She would hate me. Hell, she would kill me on the spot.

"Okay? You seemed so startled," she said as she continued to stare at me slightly distressed.

"Lexi, really, I'm okay," I lied as I hugged her. "Thanks. I can always count on you."

She patted me on the back. "Okay, no need to get cheesy."

Releasing her from the hug, I gave her another smile and headed back toward the camp. At least, I was no longer oblivious. I actually believed the lie I told everyone. I actually thought that I could possibly be a hero. I hated myself. I knew I had to go talk to Qadir now. Maybe I could get him to stop all of this and tell him I made a mistake.

Many people believe my power to turn living things into Twilight creatures and control them is immune to gods, but only a few knew that Qadir is a Twilight creature now himself. He gave up his sanity when he devoted his life to me. I twisted him into the demented bastard he is now. I ended up doing that to anyone who fell for me. Yeah, that's right. Qadir was in love with me. It was gross as hell, but I used it to my advantage. I couldn't control Qadir because he was a god, so that's how I controlled him—by twisting his emotions and thoughts and causing him to want nothing but my happiness.

But you see, I don't get happy, not after I received the force of destruction, devastation, and corruption. I was literally created to immoral everyone who came into my path; however, I always fought that even if I was a sick deranged bastard. I still cared about Lexi, Caroline, Bridget, Griffin, and all the others. I refused to corrupt them. I failed with one of them, and Griffin knew everything. Griffin was even helping me. How could he help me? I'm basically destroying his home.

"Mason!" Lexi shouted and ran after me. "You remember now, so you know how to stop Qadir," she said.

I kept walking a bit faster, not wanting to talk to her anymore. I had to figure out what I was going to do. Was I going to finish what I started? No, I couldn't. I was not going back to being a monster.

"Do you know what he's planning?" she continued to question me.

I was feeling very overwhelmed. "Go away!" I snapped.

She stopped in her tracks. "Something's wrong. Why did you lie to me?"

"I-I didn't lie to you. You just keep asking me questions, and I want you to shut up," I stated.

"Doesn't mean you get to yell at me." Lexi glared. "Stop being so grouchy."

"You have no right to say that to me. I mean, come on, have you met you?"

She was being a hypocrite. She was the grouchiest person I knew. This was odd, considering she was supposed to be the sorceress of Light and all things good in the world. You'd think she'd be this super happy girl, a typically giddy teenager. I suppose this proves that even people who appear happy might not be. People who have every reason to be happy could be suffering on the inside. Now that I thought about it, she's miserable because of me. I do that to a lot of people, whether I wanted to or not. That's just the effect I had ever since I got my powers. I wasn't born with the power of the Twilight, the power of corruption, and darkness. My father, Alash the God aka sorcerer of Death of the Realms, forced me to take control of the force of darkness. This was forbidden due to the negative impact it would have on the world. My father said that's why I was born, so I can take that power and kill all of whom he despised. Any normal demigod wouldn't have been able to contain the Twilights power, so he made sure I wasn't a demigod.

He seduced my mother, Melanie, the goddess of life, and she fell in love with him. Once I was born, he took me from her, and she never saw me again. He raised me to be able to withstand the power, so when I was ready, I could control the light as well and be unstoppable. Little did he know that over time, he was the one I wanted to kill since he tortured and abused me. I was just his secret weapon that he planned to use against his brother Castrin and the rest of the gods. When my mother found out what Alash had planned, she was furious, so she did what he did to her and seduced him to get another child, Lexi. A child who would save the entire world—even me. My parents were screwed up especially my father. What I never understood was why I still loved my father even after what he did to me. I wanted to make him proud. I wanted him to care about me, but he never did.

I met Lexi when I was eight. That was the night my father was forcing me to absorb the force of the Twilight. That was the day when I slowly started to go insane. That's what the Twilight did after all, slowly make people lose their minds.

"I'm going back to the others," Lexi sighed and was about to walk off.

Out of nowhere, Qadir walked into our view. Immediately, we both froze in our tracks. Qadir walked right up to me as if it were nothing.

"So, you remember everything?" He smirked.

"Okay, really? How did you know so fast? That like just happened," I sassed.

"I have eyes all over this place. I know where you all are twenty-four seven," he told me.

"And we are not dead already because?" I continued to sass as he was the last person I wanted to see right now.

"You know why. Don't pretend you don't," Qadir sneered.

I shot a glare at him. "Oh, shut up."

"Why are you here?" Lexi asked.

"I came to let Mason know that I have been thinking. The deal is off. I want to be in control of everything, not destroy it all." Qadir smirked. glanced at Lexi for a second, then back at me.

Lexi glared at me right then. "What the hell does he mean?" Her tone was viscous. "What deal?"

"Um, I kind of uh..."I took a deep breath and looked Lexi right in the eyes. "I planned this all. I created the Twilight to destroy everyone in the Realms. I recruited Qadir, and basically, everything that has been happening was my idea," I confessed. "I don't want to be a part of this anymore though. I want to stop what I started."

Lexi's eyes widened. She swung right at me and socked me in the face. "You bastard! Why would you do this to our home!? To everyone we love?! To me!?"

It took me awhile to process the punch as my head jerked back and caused me to crash to the ground.

"You lied to all of us!"

Qadir began to laugh, "I'd hate to break this little argument. After all, it's hilarious. However, I do not like it when people hurt my things." He walked right up to Lexi and grabbed her by the throat.

"Lexi!" I yelled and shot up. I could feel blood dripping down my nose with a fat lip somewhat forming. Lunging at Qadir was no use though. He simply used magic to make me go flying into a tree. Once my head went slamming into it, I blacked out.

There was a distant voice, a sweet silvery toned one. Caroline. I slowly opened my eyes, and she was sitting right above me, trying to get me to wake up with Bridget and Griffin looking over her shoulders.

"Mason? Mason, can you hear me?"

"Where is Lexi?" I mumbled. I bolted up and looked around in panic. "Where's Lexi?!"

She was nowhere to be seen. Qadir must have taken her, maybe even killed her. No, he would've had to have my element stone...which I hid far away. That's how you kill a god in this world. Find their opposite element stone and use it to destroy them. But all of them are very hard to find. Each god sends off in anywhere in time and space—somewhere hidden and undetectable. Mine was somewhere Qadir would never think of, the 70s. I hate the 70s. In the Realms, the 70s was much like the way it was in the regular world. Horrible. Everyone saying groovy and dressing in the most unfashionable clothes I have ever seen. Qadir wouldn't think about that time period because I tend to avoid things I hate. Also, where my element stone is hidden is totally unpredictable. You get my point.

"She wasn't at the camp. Did she come out here with you?" Griffin asked with concern all over his face.

"Qadir has her," I told them, knowing it was entirely my fault.

CHAPTER NINE:

Uncovered

"What do you mean Qadir has her?!" Griffin snapped. His rage was at an all-time high. "You let him take Lexi?!" He was probably more mad at me than the others, considering he knew I should have control over Qadir.

I would have to explain to him that Qadir just went haywire.

"It wasn't his fault Griffin." Caroline scowled at him. She helped me to my feet and hugged me. "Don't worry, Mason. It'll be okay. We will get her back."

I hugged Caroline back, not wanting her to know that Griffin was right. Why did I ever lie to her? Why did I put her through this? I was so selfish, so stupid. And Lexi, poor Lexi, was going to die or be locked up. I was going to have to find her. It was risky because if I go anywhere near Qadir, he could tell everyone about my secret. He could tell everyone I was the reason this all started. I couldn't have that. They all would hate me. They would look at me with the same hatred that Lexi had.

"What happened to your face?" Bridget asked. She was always the one who asked the random questions.

"I flew into a tree and blacked out... It must be from that," I lied.

"Mason, can I talk to you alone for a bit?" Griffin asked. He was obviously still pissed.

I just nodded and followed him away from everyone else. "What is it?" I asked.

"You promised that she wouldn't get hurt," Griffin stated.

"I know I did, and she won't," I told him. "Qadir just went against everything. He broke our deal."

"So, he is really the enemy now?" Griffin questioned.

I nodded. "Yeah, and I don't want to be on the wrong side anymore. I want to protect the world."

"That's good, but it's too late for many lives... Hopefully, Lexi won't be included," Griffin said. "Does she know what you've done?"

"Yeah, she knows I lied. That I am to blame for everything. That this was my little game to relieve my boredom," I said. "I'm so mad at myself. What was I thinking?"

Griffin frowned with guilt. "I should've warned you what would happen instead of just going along with what you wanted."

"I'm sorry, Griffin. It's not your fault."

I assured him that was Griffin's fatal flaw; he was too loyal—especially to me. See, the story I told you before about how I saved Griffin wasn't totally off. I guess Qadir shaped my mind to give me a childhood memory in Leadville. I met Bridget before I had ever met Griffin. Bridget's cousin, Alexis, was stalking one of my best friends, Trent Jones, a knight of the Sanctuary. I had never spoken to either of them before; however, Trent got sick of being followed everywhere by Alexis, so he finally told her to stop in the nicest way he could. He was a man of honor. He always tried to be polite and use his manners, so breaking a girl's heart was the last thing he wanted to do. Alexis started crying, and that's when Bridget came over and saw the whole thing. We were all around thirteen, so it was all pretty stupid. Bridget started yelling at Trent, telling him how insensitive he was and how she was going to destroy him by hanging him off the side of a cliff and letting vultures gripe his guts. Then I started yelling at Bridget and told her to leave the poor guy alone, and we ended up yelling at each other.

Now, I know what you are thinking. How am I such good friends with Bridget now? Simple. As we were yelling, I didn't know what else to say. So, I just shouted pineapple, and she just stopped without a word. I thought she was going to punch me, but she just laughed. We talked and became best friends. To this day, I call Bridget pine, and she calls me apple. And together, we are the pineapple, otherwise known as the best friendship ever created. I know its super dorky, but everyone has dorky things they do with their friends. So, yeah, after a week after first meeting Bridget, she invited me over to her house where she lived with Danny. See, I got rid of Danny and sent him to Leadville, so when Bridget and Griffin came to bring me home to the Realms, they had to face him again.

Once I first got to her house, everything seemed normal. She didn't have a mother either, so I related a lot to her, and I related even more when I found out her mother was a goddess too. Her mother is Samantha, goddess of thieves and many other things I never really paid attention to. Bridget and Griffin were demigods, which were rare in the Realms. The Sonyin sorcerers never really liked to have children, and after Lexi was born, they were forbidden from having any with each other. It was my fault really since I was forced to absorb the power of destruction, devastation, and corruption by my father, Alash. Being a child of two gods should make you immortal, and it does, but you're not born with special powers. No sorcerer is. They are just able to take control over an element that best suits you. This is my problem. The power I absorbed fits with no one, and that's why there is usually never a God of corruption here.

The sorcerers almost never find a mortal to mate with. I'm surprised Danny was selected. However, Bridget said Danny wasn't always like that. He used to be a leader of some band of thieves that would rob the royalty of the land and keep it. He was rich fast, but Matt eventually recruited him for the royal assassins, offering him more money than he ever could steal. Naturally, Danny took the deal and went there. I was surprised that I hadn't met Bridget earlier. This was before Griffin was born. Danny was a wonderful man until a few weeks after Griffin was, and he went on a mission for Matt in Blackwood. That's where he lost his heart. And by heart, I mean any sort of love, happiness, and care he could feel. Emilia's mother, that vampire from before, was the goddess of misery Katerina. She was the one who took it from him. He became a scum bag within a few hours. It didn't help that he found out Griffin wasn't his son. Griffin had no idea whom his father was and still has no clue.

Danny had always resented Griffin and hated that he had to take care of him. Griffin had no idea that Danny wasn't his real father as he was growing up, so Danny's hatred toward him just hurt him more than it would if he knew the truth. He would take his anger out on Griffin. He'd beat him and basically do what he did to him in Leadville but worse. Griffin grew up with that. He grew up thinking that all the abuse was his fault, but it wasn't. It was never the child's fault if a parent or their guardian hurt them. Never. So, he resorted to drugs and other addicting things that I strongly advise against. Bridget couldn't get him off them. Every time she tried, he would just lash out at her. He was at the lowest point of his life. He was so sad. Just thinking about what he went through made me depressed.

I met him that day, the first time I went to Bridget's house. He was fighting with Danny, of course, and I saw Danny smack him right across the face right when I entered their living room. Bridget was so horrified that I saw her father hurt her little brother, she apologized and immediately tried to get me out of the house. Danny began to hurt Griffin more, pinned him to the ground, and kept punching him. I, being an immortal, all powerful god of destruction at the time, went right up to Danny and threw him off of Griffin right through their wall. That was the moment Bridget and Griffin found out what I was, who I was. I never really liked telling people I was the prince of the Sanctuary, let alone a god, one of the Sonyin Sorcerers.

Bridget freaked out at first but laughed her butt off at Danny's unconscious body outside on their lawn. I threw him so hard that he almost knocked a tree down. He almost died, which I wasn't upset about. Griffin ran off before I could even talk to him, but I found him later in the graveyard near by the Sanctuary. He was high as hell, and that's when I decided to make him stop. It was hard at first, but I let him move in at the castle with me along with Bridget, and eventually, we got him off the drugs. So, ever since then, Griffin, for some reason, felt like he owed me something. He didn't, but I did enjoy his friendship. I could always count on him. When I needed him, he would always be there. But I eventually steered him wrong, and now, I felt like a monster.

"We have to go get her. Qadir needs to learn his place," Griffin said. "He shouldn't have crossed you."

"So, what do you say? Bridget, you, and I go to save Lexi?" I questioned.

He nodded. "I won't let him get away with this. Let's show Qadir who's boss in this world."

"Me?" I asked.

"You," he said.

"Cute, really. You two always were so close," Qadir said from behind us.

"Okay, seriously?!" I shouted at him as I turned to face him with rage.

"What?" he questioned.

Griffin didn't hesitate. He quickly shoved Qadir into the tree, putting a knife up next to his neck. "Where is she?"

"Feisty. I like it," Qadir chuckled. He vanished and reappeared by me, putting his arm around my shoulder. "I want to make a deal with you, Mason. You can have you sister back if you do what I say, got it?"

I pushed him away from me and glared. "No way."

"Just one little deal, or your sister will be lost forever," Qadir said.

"What are you going to do to her?" Griffin puffed.

"I will rip her to shreds and send each different limb of hers into a different time and place throughout the universe. It will take you centuries to return her to her complete self, so I suggest you take the deal." Qadir smiled.

"What's the deal?" I asked, disgusted by the image he just put in my head.

"I want you to kill Matthew," Qadir stated plainly.

My eyes widened. He wanted me to kill Matt!? I may hate him, or at least, pretended to...exactly. I pretended to hate Matt, but I didn't hate him. Now, I have to kill him to get Lexi back? "No!"

"Matt is a part of the family!" Griffin shouted at Qadir.

Griffin was right, we were all a big family. I betrayed them all once. I couldn't do it again.

"It's the only way to get your sister back," Qadir declared.

What was I going to do? "Don't you want anyone else dead?" I asked.

"Griffin." He smirked and giggled a bit. Like a snarky giggle, a short snarky annoying giggle that made me want to throw him across the room.

"Oh, you are just jealous I have more of a chance with Mason than you," Griffin sassed.

I laughed, and we high-fived each other as we mocked him.

Qadir rolled his eyes and made Griffin go flying back. He got right up in my face once again, backing me into a tree. "Kill Matthew. That's the deal...or at least, let me kill him."

I just glared at Qadir more than I ever had before. I couldn't hurt Matt, but I couldn't just let Lexi end up torn apart across time and space. I took a deep breath, and my gaze went to the ground. "Fine... I will let you kill Matt," I told him. "Are you happy?"

"Very happy." Qadir smirked sadistically. "Bring him tomorrow to Acantha. To the Departed Falls. I will kill him then. Do we have a deal?"

I nodded. "Yes, we have a deal."

CHAPTER TEN:

The beginning of the end

We all had been flying for a while, heading to the southern parts of Epona. I tagged along with Caroline on her dragon, Jiggles. Still hate the name. I watched the ground beneath me. The rebellion was located in the Ancient wood, which was ruled by my mother, Melanie. The goddess of life. She was locked up at Kule Palace with the other sorcerers. I managed to create an indestructible force field around it, so they couldn't escape and save the world. Kule floated above the Realms and moved from one kingdom to the next every day. It was basically a giant floating island that you only could see if you flew almost to space. They literally had a view of space from their windows.

See, the Realms is located in a different galaxy than Earth. You could say we're a planet, but we're more like a huge floating flat rock with the ability to sustain life. The Realms is a part of the Selenite Galaxy, a place so far away from the Milky Way galaxy. It's billions of years old, and many other worlds dwelled here. All similar to the Realms, just floating flat large rocks that can sustain life. It's magic, of course. This Galaxy was full of magic. There's a theory that all of the worlds in the Selenite Galaxy used to be a part of one large planet all combined. However, the gods broke it apart and separated them to create peace between one another. Could you imagine that? An entire planet where all the gods used to live together? It must've been chaotic, the most powerful beings all living together. I see why they would separate. I wasn't born in time to see it, considering I'm only eighteen. Castrin and a few of the other Sonyin sorcerers were probably there.

"Why are we going to South Epona?" I asked Caroline. "I want to go back to the rebellion. I haven't seen Matt in forever."

She looked at me confused. "You want to see Matt? And you aren't pretending to not want to?" She questioned.

I chuckled a bit. Of course, she would say something like that. After a while, we eventually reached the castle of Epona, which was where the Druids lived—a peaceful group of people who were highly respected in the Realms. The others wanted to see if the leader could help us find Lexi. Griffin and I, of course, didn't tell them we already had a plan in motion. A horrible plan but still a plan. I just needed to find a way to get Matt all the way to Acantha, one of the thirteen kingdoms of the Realms. Matt was at the rebellion, which was in the Summer lands, and I was all the way in the Spring Lands. Griffin and I were going to have to find a way to separate from the others.

"Let's do this quickly. We don't need the Twilight finding you again," Susalea announced.

"The Druids don't need to end up like the people of Seaside."

"This way just past this hill, and we'll be able to see the entire village of Epona." Ambriel smiled.

Each kingdom had one village, which was usually more like a large town, depending on the kingdom's size. She trotted up the hill. You'd think as an angel, she'd be more graceful about it, but that wasn't Ambriel. Ambriel was the weirdest angel I had ever met. She was assigned to me as my guardian angel by Castrin, and he felt I needed the extra guidance, which I clearly did. He should've sent someone better at the job. I loved Ambriel, but she didn't give a crap about whether I was doing something right or wrong. She just hung out in her room all day watching TV—yes, we have TV in the Realms—or reading. That's why everyone said how Ambriel wasn't good at her job. In a way, she was smart for not trying to make me do the right thing. I was a stubborn person, and usually when someone wanted me to do one thing, I would turn around and do the opposite. She saved herself the frustration of trying to battle me on my decisions. I loved Ambriel though. I could always go to her if I wanted to escape the drama that is my life. Most of the time, she was never involved in it, so she was a good getaway. She became my guardian angel when I was sixteen, ironically when I started this whole plan to destroy the Realms.

My plan to destroy the Realms was simple really. I was so twisted in my head that I wanted to completely kill any form of life in the entire Realms. Basically, mass genocide. Why would I want to do this? The answer very well could be that I am a crazy bipolar, psychopath, which I totally am; however, it was more than that. My entire childhood was horrible since I lived with my demented father who forced me to take control of the power of darkness. Most people thought I was born with it, and some still do, but that is just a cover so that no one knew the truth. It was torture being forced to absorb all of that evil when I was only eight. It had many years to corrupt my mind, and it succeeded. I hate myself for not being able to fight it forever.

I gave up a week after Matt took me in. I was so used to living in hell, so I let the darkness take my mind. I was lucky to escape though and foolish for not seeing it sooner. My father used to beat me practically every day. He'd lock me up in a dark room with no windows for days on end. One time, he got so angry with me that he drowned me. I would be dead because of that if I wasn't immortal. I hated my father. I felt so abused and tormented. I hated feeling so pathetic, so worthless, and so weak. I wanted everyone else to feel that way, so I no longer was alone. That's when I engaged my plan. Qadir had always been a bit obsessed with me, so like I said before, I used that to my advantage. I always felt a bit bad because the more time Qadir focused on me, the less time he would focus on his son. Now that I think about it, it was probably a good thing Qadir didn't care about his son. If he did, then he would've grown up to be just like his father.

His son's name was Pie. I know. It's really stupid, but it's not his real name. He never told me his real name. Pie was a really good friend of mine, but he was an odd guy. Pie randomly appeared all the time, and by that, I mean you would never know when he was in a room with you. He could make himself invisible and travel from place to place in the blink of an eye. I guess it helped with his favorite activity, which was to cause mischief. His mischief wasn't anything too bad. He would just pull small pranks all the time like putting itching powder in people's underwear. He was smart enough to never do that to me though. He knew he would die if he did. Pie was a hilarious nut job. Also, he has a huge crush on Bridget, so he tended to prank her a lot as a way of trying to get her to notice him. She always pranked him back as she was the queen of pranks and schooled him every time. Honestly, I wish they would just date already.

Caroline took my hand as we followed Ambriel up the hill to get a view of the village. I glanced at her and smiled a bit. She smiled back. Her smile made my heart melt. Honestly, she was the best thing that ever happened to me, and she made the pain go away. I just wanted to hug her right then, but it would be hard to walk. And I wasn't really one who liked showing affection in front of other people. The trolls were bickering behind us, not carrying if it was annoying anyone—especially me. Bridget and Susalea followed closely behind, talking about something. Griffin was a few feet away from the group, probably worrying about Lexi. He must really love her. I'm glad she had such a great guy who liked her. Griffin was an amazing person. Everyone I knew was amazing, so why didn't I think about how I would hurt them before I started all of this?

Ambriel froze once she reached the top of the hill. I grew confused. She looked horrified. I finally reached her and looked out at the view of the town. The Twilight creatures were everywhere, guarding the borders of the village. Soldiers had people lined up with whips in their hands, and occasionally, I heard a few yells and whip on of the workers with it. It was awful, just awful. Eventually, I processed that the workers were the Druids. Qadir had them enslaved, forcing them to do who knows what. I lost it. How could Qadir do this? This was slavery obviously. Qadir was playing the game with his own set of rules now. So much for controlling that jerk.

"What do we do?" Caroline questioned with devastation in her tone. "We have to help them."

"There's not much we can do, There are too many of them," Griffin said.

"But—" Caroline tried to debate, but I cut her off.

"He's right. With the Twilight and the soldiers, we wouldn't stand a chance," I told her. "And the Druids wouldn't help fight. They're pacifists."

"Then what do we do?!" Caroline snapped. "We can't just leave them here."

"Look. We aren't heroes, Caroline. We can't save everyone we come across," I argued.

"If we aren't the heroes, then who is?" She asked. "Someone has to save them. No one else will."

"If we are the heroes, then we're the worst group of heroes ever," Bridget remarked.

I looked at her. "Thank you, Bridget, for that uplifting comment," I said sarcastically.

"Just stating a fact." She defended herself.

"She's right. We are horrible heroes," Ambriel agreed.

"I don't even classify as a hero." I grimaced.

"Mason, you're the biggest hero out of all of us," Caroline said.

Griffin, Bridget, and I just started laughing. Caroline glared at us, scrunching up her nose like a bunny. She looked adorable.

"I'm sorry Caroline, but I'm no hero."

"Yeah, of course, you aren't." She ran off back into the woods. As she ran off, I watched her, suddenly feeling bad. I ran after her. It took me awhile to find her, but eventually I was able to locate Caroline. She was crying by a meadow. I walked over to her and sat down. "Caroline?"

She didn't look at me. In fact, she seemed to shield herself more as I sat down.

"I'm sorry if I upset you."

"It's not you. It's everything that's happening... It all seems so hopeless," she choked.

"I know," I sighed. "It's simple honestly. I can easily take away the Twilight from Qadir's control, and Lexi could easily destroy me and it. I meant it."

"You are not taking back your power. It will destroy you," she said. "And I know what you meant. The only way to destroy it is to kill you."

"Which I am sure you're against," I muttered.

"Yes, I never want to lose you," She whispered and looked up at me with her warm brown eyes. "I love you more than I have ever loved anyone."

I wrapped my arms around her and held her close to me. "I never thought I could love until I met you."

She cuddled up to me. "I love you."

"I love you too, Caroline," I whispered and wiped some tears off her face.

After a few minutes while I sat there with Caroline, Griffin came and found us. "Um, Mason... Matt he's here."

I looked at him with a worried expression. Of course, Matt was here. "We should go greet him then, shouldn't we?" I asked Caroline.

She got up. "Yeah, I know how anxious you are to see him," she teased.

I got up and kissed her. "You're hilarious. Truly." I took her hand walking off, following Griffin to the others.

I saw Matt once we reached everyone. He was talking to Bridget. Cano, Matt's under-aged wife was there. Matt was like thirty-five, and she was twenty-eight. Only a few years older than me. It wasn't illegal, but I found it weird. They had Max when Cano was around seventeen.

"Matt," I called as I walked up to him.

He looked at me. "Hey, loser. What's up?"

I rolled my eyes. He always found ways to insult me. I guess I brought it on myself. I was always a jerk to him. We never got along. He totally hated me and thought I hated him too. But I didn't. In fact, I really cared about Matt, so what Qadir wanted me to do to him was going to kill me inside. I would've said no if it weren't for Lexi being kidnapped. Matt was kind of a hero of mine because he took me and Lexi in, so we could finally live together and no longer separated by our parents. He made sure my father wasn't able to hurt me anymore. He made sure that Lexi and I were safe. He didn't know it, but Matt was a pretty decent guy when he wanted to be, and sometimes, when he didn't even try.

"So, why are you here?" I asked.

"You and Lexi disappeared on us. We set out to make sure you two were okay," he said. "I can see now that you aren't considering Lexi is missing and you look like you have just gone through hell."

"I do?" I asked confused.

"Yeah, you have cuts all over your face." Matt pointed.

"Not my face!" I panicked, totally joking. Only a few select people in this group actually knew I wasn't that self-absorbed, so the ones who thought I was being serious rolled their eyes. So, Matt, Cano, Susalea, and yeah, that's it.

"I can help clean you up." Caroline smiled.

"We don't have time to turn Mason back into his good-looking self," Ambriel said.

"He's still good looking like this," Griffin commented.

Everyone looked at him perplexed. He looked at them, feeling mortified.

I laughed a bit, "Guys, stop staring at Griffin."

"We have to save Lexi. That's obvious. We planned on asking the Druids for help, but they're no longer able to aid us," Ambriel said.

"Why can't they help?" Cano asked.

"Qadir has enslaved them," Susalea said grimly.

"We can't help, not without an army to back us up," Bridget chimed in. "Susalea sent word to the rebellion. They should be on their way."

"So, we're going to save them?" Caroline was certainly happy to hear that.

"I'll go get Lexi then. Griffin and Matt can come with me," I declared. "There's a weapon in Acantha that I could use against Qadir. We'll go fetch that and head for Lexi." The weapon was a lie. I just couldn't think of any other way to get Matt to Acantha.

"Why you three?" Bridget asked, clearly feeling left out.

"We all care about Lexi the most," I simply stated.

"Fair enough," Bridget said.

"Don't worry, Bridget. I'll stay with you," a voice said from behind us. Pie walked over to us, went right up to Bridget, and put his arm around her.

"Pie, you're here!" I smiled.

When Bridget shoved him off of her, he just vanished and reappeared next to me. "At least, someone is happy to see me." He smiled back. "I've been in Epona for a while, trying to think of a plan to save the Druids. So far, all I have done is make a few guards trip on their faces, and I also gave a few some wedgies."

"You're so immature," Griffin sighed.

"Thanks, pal," Pie said with a smug smile planted on his face.

"We need to get going. The sooner we get Lexi, the better," I said.

"Mason, I'm coming with you," Caroline declared.

"No, you aren't," I said firmly.

"I don't want to be away from you again. What if something bad happens? I would just worry," she said.

I looked at Griffin, and he shook his head no. Of course, she couldn't come. If she came, she could see us send Matt to his death. "I'll be fine. You trust me, don't you?" I took her hand and held it, getting closer to her and stroking her cheek.

She looked up at me and bit her lip. "It's not you that I don't trust. It's everyone who wants you dead. Everyone who is plotting to kill you, which, for the record, is a lot of people."

"You can stay with us, Caroline. Help us save the Druids like you wanted to," Bridget said.

Caroline began to pout at me. "Mason, please?" she begged. Her face was so cute.

"Oh, fine!" I said, being frustrated that I couldn't say no to her.

Griffin glared at me. "Well, let's get going then. The fastest way is the warpstone. It's not too far from here."

"Okay, good luck, guys," Matt said to everyone. "Let's get back the Realms one battle at a time."

I rolled my eyes and walked off. Caroline followed, holding my hand tightly and resting her head on my shoulder as we walked. Griffin gave Bridget a quick hug and ran after us. Matt, of course, was the last to follow, considering he had to make out with Cano first. Gross, I know. I loved having my memory back. I actually knew where we were heading for once, and it was pretty great. Everything seemed to be going the way I needed it to. The only thing I needed to figure out was how to get Matt in position for his murder and how to keep Caroline far from it.

We arrived in Acantha shortly after we reached the warpstone, which only took about five minutes to reach. During the entire walk, Matt was asking me about this secret weapon that I had made up. Luckily for me, I knew how to make stuff up. I told Matt that this weapon was Qadir's opposites stone that Grace, the goddess of wisdom, had hid it here. He fell for it, mainly because he had no idea that gods even had stones in the first place that could kill other gods. The only person who knew I was lying was Griffin. Even Caroline fell for my lie about the secret weapon. Acantha was a nice place and was known for its farming and sarsaparilla soft drink, which they called sweet water.

"All right, where is this secret weapon of yours, lover boy?" Matt asked.

"Why must you call me lover boy?" I sighed in frustration.

"Because I can, and it suits you," Matt stated.

"No, it doesn't. I don't love anyone but Caroline," I argued.

"Exactly. Caroline and Mason sitting in a tree," he began to sing, but I quickly covered his mouth, and he flicked me in the head.

I was about to punch him in the face when Caroline pulled me away from him.

"Let's get searching, Mason. Lead the way," Caroline said.

"Oh, right. About the secret weapon. Only two people can enter the river where it's hidden, and we all know how I am with water," I told them. Making this up was getting too easy, which could also mean my story wasn't believable. It probably wasn't.

"So, Matt and I will go. You and Caroline, keep watch," Griffin said. "Come on, Matt. The river should be this way," he spoke and headed down the path.

"I'll meet up with you soon. Hold on," Matt said. "Caroline, can I talk to Mason alone?"

This was it. Oh, crap. He knew. He knew I was lying, and he was going to ask me what was really going on. "Why?" I quickly asked before Caroline could respond.

"I need to talk to you about something," Matt stated.

"I'll be waiting for you at the farmers market," Caroline told me and walked off.

My gaze focused on Matt after I watched her leave. "What is it?"

"Look. Everything seems to be going to shit lately," Matt began. "I mean crap. Sorry. I didn't mean to swear in front of you, kid."

"I'm not a kid anymore, Matt. I don't care if you swear," I told him.

He always tried to refrain from cussing in front of Lexi, me, and Max. But he was very bad at it. He would throw f-bombs around all the time and say so many words I disliked. He had the mouth of a sailor. At first, he didn't bother censoring himself, but Lexi got older and told him to f off. He realized the error of his ways. She still says it sometimes—only when she is really mad. It's partly my fault because when she first said the f word, I high fived her because she said it to Matt.

"You will always be that ten-year-old boy who came to live with me eight years ago," Matt said. "I miss when you were a kid. You were a lot easier to handle."

"Was I?" I asked, trying to get him to second guess himself. I was a horrible child, so I don't know what he was talking about.

"Yeah, we used to play together all the time," he began. "Do you remember that time when I first taught you how to play with a gun, and you almost shot one of the guards in the head?" he asked with a small smile and chuckled a little. "Hilarious."

Matt wasn't the most responsible guardian I could have gotten, forget the guard I almost shot with that pistol. I was ten when that happened. Who gives a ten-year-old a gun? Matt does; that's who.

"Can you just get to the point of this conversation please?" I questioned.

He looked at me sadly and sighed, "I just wanted to say that no matter what happens, we can get through this. We are all a family. You, me, Cano, Lexi and Max... Even if Max is dead."

Wrong. Max wasn't dead at all. I had Qadir lock him up somewhere that he couldn't escape from. Max knew what I was up to. He was a super genius, so he figured it out easily. I had to exterminate him, but I loved him. So, I just locked him up and told Matt that Qadir killed him, Matt's only real son. Technically, his only son. I didn't count, nor do I think Matt even saw me as his son. Max was the most adorable eleven-year-old ever. I personally hate kids, so I never really found any child adorable. He looked just like Matt but smaller and actually cute. He had these big purple eyes, which he got from Cano and tan skin with black messy skater hair. He was a happy little kid but also smarter than me. How could an eleven-year-old with Matt and Cano's genes be smarter than me?

"Okay, great talk. Now go catch up with Griffin. Lexi can't wait any longer," I said and tried to push him in the direction I wanted him to go.

"Hold on!" Matt shouted and stepped out of the way.

I almost crashed to the ground if he didn't stop me. I looked up at him as I processed what just happened.

"Mason, I'm worried that I will never see you again just like I may never see Lexi again."

"Don't say that," I told him. Though he was right if the plan went the way I hoped. Then he would never see Lexi or anyone else again.

This was when something unexpected happened. He hugged me. I was utterly shocked. He never hugged me before. He didn't care about me, so why was he saying all of this crap?

"Stay safe. I can't lose anyone else to that bastard, Qadir."

Oh, come on! Now, I felt guiltier than I've been before. I forced myself out of his grip. "I can handle myself." I swiftly headed to Caroline who was looking at farmers' stands.

Before I could even reach Caroline, I was pulled off into the nearest group of trees before I could even blink. I was pinned to the ground by the infamous blonde vampire, Emilia.

"Hey, babe." She smirked.

"How many times do I have to tell you? I am not your babe." I rolled my eyes.

She sat on my stomach, releasing her grip on my shoulders. "You use to be." She pouted.

"No, Emilia. I was forced to be with you before, not willingly," I reminded her.

"That didn't stop you from sleeping with me, which was kind of a mixed signal," Emilia said and slapped me. "Jerk."

"Ow." I glared as my cheek stung from her slap.

"Usually, vampires pick a mate for life. I picked you, and you tossed me under the rug like I was nothing for that girl," Emilia said.

"Can you get off of me?" I asked.

Emilia was the princess of Blackwood. Matt thought it would be a good idea to get them on our side considering Emilia's family was the most ruthless royals in all the Realms. So, Matt arranged a marriage between her and me. It was horrible. All she wanted to do was spend time with me. She practically stalked me, so I used it to my advantage, I guess. I feel bad for it now; no one should be used like that. Emilia also works for Qadir now most likely, but she is still obsessed with me. Maybe, I could get her and her kingdom on my side once again.

"I hear you're a good boy now, saving the day. Well, trying to at least," She giggled. "Good doesn't suit you, Mason."

"Then what does?" I asked.

She then came close to my face, almost close enough to kiss me. "Me. Don't you remember how perfect we were together?" she whispered. "The havoc we set on this land. We were unstoppable."

"I love Caroline. I've been dating her for two years now. Get over me." I glared.

She shot up and threw me into a tree. "You're supposed to love me!" she yelled and stormed at me.

My eyes widened, and I pulled out a knife in my belt as if it would actually do much, but I had to fight back this time. I quickly stabbed her in her stomach, which threw her off just enough for me to get up and run. I bolted, but of course, vampires were faster than humans. Emilia caught me in no time. I fought back. But before I knew it, Qadir appeared and smirked. Emilia let go of me and walked over to him. I looked at Qadir. This was it. Matt was dead; he just had to be.

"Emilia, let's not kill our friend," Qadir told her.

"I'm not your friend...did you do it? Can I have my sister back?" I questioned.

Qadir kept that stupid smirk on his face. "I'm keeping Lexi actually. Considering I didn't follow through with the deal."

I sneered. But a part of me was relieved that Matt wasn't dead. "Why would you back out of the deal?! I shouldn't have trusted you. Jokes on you though. Matt's still alive, and we can find Lexi before you can hurt her," I told him angrily.

"Well, I would've killed Matt, but he wasn't at the river where I was waiting," he said, not meeting my gaze until he spoke again. "I had to take someone else's life in his place."

"What?" My eyes widened, and I darted off toward the river.

I heard Qadir's laughter all around me. The only one at the river was Griffin. Was Griffin dead now? Oh, gods, please say he wasn't dead. It felt as though it took me hours to reach the river. I ran so fast that I was almost out of breath. I could see Griffin's body resting by the river. My heart fell as I ran up to him. I checked his pulse, and he was still breathing. So then, who died? I froze. Caroline...

I looked around in panic. She couldn't be dead, not her. Anyone but her! I felt a huge knot in my stomach as I got closer to the river, which was red. There was loud ringing in my ears, and the world seemed to move slower. I looked down at the clear river of Acantha through the murky red fog of blood flowing through the water. I saw her body at the bottom of the river with a large rock placed on her chest. This had to be some sick nightmare.

"Caroline!?" I screamed out as tears poured from my eyes.

Normally, I would've been against this, but I dove right into the water and swam to her the best I could, trying to fight the current of the river. I pushed the rock off of her and pulled her out of the water, setting her down on the emerald grass. She was so cold with her skin pale white. Her lips were purple, and she had no pulse. No sign of life.

"Caroline, please wake up," I cried.

I never felt so destroyed. I was about to try to get the water out of her lungs, but when I inspected her further, I noticed her chest was ripped open. It was gruesome. There was no way to bring her back. He took her heart. Qadir ripped her heart out. I started cry even more. I couldn't control it. The more I cried, the more real this was. How could I have let this happen?

"Caroline, please don't leave me," I whispered as I held her close to me. She lay motionless in my arms. "I love you. I love you," I spoke softly. "Please stop being dead." Looking down at her face was torture. It was so lifeless. She wasn't smiling back at me like she used to. She wasn't there to tell me I was going to be okay. I never felt so broken before, so destroyed.

CHAPTER ELEVEN:

Broken

September

October

November

December

January

February

…March

CHAPTER TWELVE:

The search

It had been months since Caroline died. I hadn't been the same since. After I buried her, I disappeared before anyone I knew could find me. They had no idea where I was for months now, and I had no idea if they were still alive. I felt bad. I should have saved Lexi. For all I know, Qadir could've killed her by now. I always felt as though I should go back to everyone, but then I remembered that if I do, I would most likely get them all killed.

September 28th, 2014. That's when Caroline died. Today is March 1st, 2015, and my birthday was two days away. March 3rd. This was the first birthday in a long time that I would be spending alone. I didn't care though. Becoming nineteen wasn't a big deal to me anyway. Not when Caroline wasn't there with me.

I would never be able to move on from her death. She was everything to me.

I had no idea what state the Realms was in. I was too far in the middle of nowhere to know. As much as I hated the desert, I went to Onyx Valley, the black desert of the Sacred Grove. It was just miles of black sand and a crystal blue sky. At night, you literally couldn't see anything. No one lived this far out in the desert. Onyx Valley was a part of the Autumn Lands surprisingly, considering it was the warmest kingdom in the Realms. The black sand really attracted heat. Unless you were the native people, stepping in the sand shoe-less was a bad idea. The natives of Onyx Valley were big-footed Dwarves. They all had beards, even the women. The women grew the biggest beards and were the toughest of their kind.

I was living in one of my escape house that I had in every kingdom. Only I knew where they were. I took Jiggles, Caroline's dragon, and just flew out here to get away. But Jiggles left a month ago. Sitting on my couch alone, I was reading a book about some young wizard who went to a magical school and crap happened. Caroline always wanted me to read them. I wasn't fond of reading, but she wanted me to, so I was. It was a great story so far, but I was only a few chapters into the first book. There were a lot of them. It was her favorite book. I set the book on the side table and took a deep breath. Things were so hard to do. I just wanted to sit there and do nothing, but I always tried to do something, so I would seem normal. It was a weird thing I did. I never could just sit and take in the moment. If I wasn't doing something, I felt like someone would get mad at me. Even now, that was the case, and I was alone. Why was I so weird?

I heard loud scratching on the door downstairs. My eyes widened, and I shot up. Suddenly, a series of grating barks followed the scratching, and I realized who it was. I sprinted to the door almost tripping on the stairs. Flinging the door open, I peered down at the little dog, Sparky. He looked dreadful with his fur was all matted and super skinny. I was a horrible owner. He jumped with excitement, and his little tongue stuck out as he made little whining noises of happiness. I picked him up.

"How did you find me?" I wondered.

He always seemed to be able to find his way back to me. I was going to have to look into this. Carrying him to the bathroom, I grabbed an electric razor and started shaving off the mats from his fur. I petted him, so he wouldn't freak out too much. He hated being shaved. He began to fight me a bit, but I held him down. I refused to let him stay in this state any longer. After I finished getting Sparky back into a nice clean state, I took him to the kitchen and gave him water. Boy, was he thirsty. I was shocked he survived out in that heat for so long. His poor little paws were burnt, so he didn't stand. I felt so bad for this poor dog. Maybe if I brought him to a medic in the village, they could heal him with some magical healing spell. Then he wouldn't be so tortured as he walked. I watched him gulp down the water. It was a huge relief to have him with me again. I loved this dog more than I loved basically everything. He made me feel less depressed just by being here, my little miracle dog. He would go to the ends of the universe to be by my side, and he proved that when he arrived at my door.

Once he finished his food, I took him to my bedroom and set him on the bed, so he could get some sleep. We cuddled up together, but I was careful of his paws. In no time, he was fast asleep. I held him close and eventually drifted off myself. I was surrounded by darkness, so the only light I had was a torch that burned bright with a blue flame. I appeared to be in a cave. Something seemed familiar about this place. It was the Caverns, the caves by the castle in the Sanctuary. Lexi and I would always go there to get away for a bit. Ironically, it was also the way to get to Morena, our father Alash's kingdom.

"Mason," a voice spoke softly from behind me.

I turned around, and Lexi stood there staring at me. "Lexi?"

"We need to talk...now," she said.

"This is just a dream. You aren't really here," I said, mostly to myself.

"No, Mason, it's not entirely a dream," Lexi said. "I needed to speak with you. I've been locked up for some months now. I assume you don't have a plan to save me since I'm still here."

"Sorry... I'm not really with everyone right now," I confessed.

"So, you haven't even been trying to save me?!" she asked, sounding offended.

"I'm sorry. Something happened," I told her.

"What could possibly have happened for you to leave everyone we care about, let me rot here for months, and avoid your duties to the Realms?! After what you did, after what you caused, you have no right to just hide away!" she shouted with rage-filled eyes.

"Caroline died... Qadir killed her," I said, saying the words made me want to vomit. It was too painful.

Lexi's face fell, and suddenly, I was pulled into a hug. "I'm so sorry, Mason."

I hugged her back, trying not to tear up and said nothing.

"When did she die?" she asked.

"Not long after you were taken," I said.

She let me go and sighed, "If I had known, I wouldn't have yelled at you," she said. "But it's been months now, Mason. It's time to get out there and save the Realms. It's probably gotten worse since you went MIA."

"I know it is," I said. "But I wouldn't have changed anything. I'm useless. I don't have powers like you anymore. I can't do much. You got kidnapped, and Qadir is just getting stronger. I tried to get you back by killing Matt only to have the love of my life die instead, and I started all of this because I got bored and decided to play a game involving the lives of everyone in the world. So many are dead because of me. I have no right to save it, and I couldn't if I tried. I'd just make it worse."

"You're the only one who can undo all of this. I will help you, but I can't locked up," Lexi spoke gently and looked at me. Her eyes were hopeful, and I could just feel the inspirational speech coming on. "You can save us. It may have been your fault for most of what happened. Caroline wouldn't want you to not try, Mason. You don't need to have powers to be a hero. Isn't that what Caroline wanted? For you to see yourself as the hero that you are?"

She was right for once. Caroline saw me as a hero. I didn't know why, but she always saw the best in me. I couldn't let her down. I had to destroy Qadir once and for all. "What's your plan? You have one right? Or did you just expect me to think of it?"

She smiled a bit. "Yeah, I had an idea," she said. "To save the Realms for good, Qadir has to die."

"You want to kill Qadir?" I questioned.

"Who doesn't?" she said. "It's simple. All we have to do is find the element stone of Grace, goddess of wisdom. If we find that, we can use it to kill him."

"Grace is a genius, and her stone is the hardest to find," I told her.

"I'm sure if we asked Grace, she would tell us in order to stop Qadir," Lexi said.

"Problem. I may have had the gods locked up before we went to Leadville," I confessed. "They're all behind an unbreakable force field in their palace, Kule."

"You trapped the sorcerers!?" Lexi freaked.

"Yes, I'm surprised they haven't been able to break out yet. I guess that shows how powerful darkness is," I said. "Speaking of darkness, Qadir still has my powers. Even if we have the stone, he could just get the Twilight to stop us."

"Don't change the subject mister! What the hell were you thinking?!" Lexi raged. "Every time you tell me more and more about what you did, I just get angrier at you."

"I'm sorry I am an idiot. I don't know what else to tell you." I rolled my eyes.

"I hate you...not really, but I am mad at you," she blabbed. "No, I do hate you. No, I don't."

"Can you shut up?" I asked sarcastically.

She glared at me. "No! I will cut off your limbs and feed them to wolves!"

My eyes widened. "Lexi, breathe. We need to figure out what we're going to do. It won't be long before I wake up."

She continued to glare at me but took a deep breath. "Okay, here's the plan."

CHAPTER THIRTEEN:

Knowing

What Lexi and I had to do was simple. Get her out of Qadir's custody, kill Qadir, and stop the destruction of the Realms. One thing I knew for sure was that Qadir wanted the entire world for himself. He wanted everyone to die aside from him and a select few. Him, Emilia, and me. The rest of mankind was to be slaughtered one kingdom at a time. He already got Seaside, which was all I knew for now. Hopefully, the other kingdoms were still alive.

The Sanctuary, my home. The strongest kingdom in the Realms. I gave that one to Qadir. Hopefully, he didn't kill everyone in my kingdom yet. Maybe, I could save them. The Sanctuary was located in the center of the Realms apart of the Summer lands, but a small section of it was in the Spring lands. A large river circled around the kingdom with two large waterfalls on the eastern and western points of the river. Magic flowed in the water, considering it continued to flow yet. There was no entrance or exit for the water. Qadir was going to taint it with darkness, and I had to stop him. For the Realms, but more importantly, for Caroline.

I remembered that conversation I had with Susalea when I first got back to the Realms. She told me what she thought Qadir was planning. I blew it, but now I remembered I was planning to harness that power myself to destroy all of the gods. The older I got, the stronger the power became. In two days, I'd be nineteen, and the Twilight would get stronger. I still didn't fully understand it. My father said I was born to control this darkness, but every time I tried, it just drove me to insanity, depression, and misery. I didn't want that anymore; just look what it has done to Qadir. He used to be kind, but I used my power to destroy any good in him. Now he's just...one of my victims. This was all my fault. Sighing, I headed downstairs, nearly having a heart attack as I saw a little boy playing with Sparky.

"Mason," the boy said and stood up, facing me.

"Max?" I questioned and looked at his face. "It is you...but how?"

"Qadir let me go. He said he didn't need me anymore," he told me. "Then he brought me here."

"Wait. He knew where I was the entire time, didn't he?" I asked as a bitter feeling filled my gut. He always knew where I was no matter where I went. But how?

"Does it matter? We have some catching up to do," Max stated with his tone angry. He clearly wasn't here on good terms.

"Yes, it matters, Max. He's playing with me," I sneered.

"The same way you were playing with everyone else?" he asked.

"I...Max, you smell horrible. Did he ever let you bathe?" I didn't mean to change the subject, but his scent was so horrible.

"He would let me bathe every once in a while, but I haven't in a few weeks. So what?" Max glared. He was clearly trying to act tough. He was normally a really nice kid. I got on his bad side, so I wasn't going to be treated very kindly.

"Go upstairs and shower. I'll see if I have any clothes that will fit you, but I probably don't," I told him.

Max sighed and ran his hand through his ratted thick black hair, getting his fingers caught in them. "Ow," he cried under his breath.

"Okay. First, we need to brush your hair. Possibly cut it... I'm sorry I did this to you." I frowned and walked over to him.

"No, you're not." He continued to glare.

Sighing, I picked him up and threw him over my shoulder. I held my breath, so I couldn't smell him and carried him to the bathroom.

"Let me go!" he shouted at me and started kicking.

I ignored him. I also didn't argue back because in order to speak, I'd have to breathe in his horrid stench. I set him down, grabbed a brush, and began to work on terminating all the mats in his hair. First, Sparky, and now, Max. What was I some sort of groomer?

He winced in pain. "Why are you being so nice to me?" he asked as I continued to brush his hair.

"You're my brother, and I made a mistake, hurting you terribly," I told him. "I really am sorry Max, but I've changed since you last saw me."

"Is that because Qadir has you powers?" Max asked. "I know what they do to you. They make you insane and evil."

"Yeah, I never could control them, could I?" I sighed.

"It's probably because you would always get so wrapped up in feeling bad for yourself that you never opened your eyes and saw that you had so many reasons to stay grounded. For example, you had a family. Sure, it wasn't the ideal family, but it was still a family. You pushed us away. You had friends who would do anything and everything for you, yet you didn't care and even used one of them for your revenge plot. If people find out about this, Griffin's going to get blamed too. And let's not forget Caroline. You had Caroline, yet you didn't care. You still felt like you needed to prove something."

I glared at the child. Sometimes, he didn't know when to shut up. I quickly brushed out the last knot a bit violently, causing Max to cry out in more pain. Then I dropped the brush and walked out of the bathroom. "Take a bath, Max," I ordered him and went down to check on Sparky.

My heart ached from Max's words. He was right. I pushed my family away, I treated my friends like they were nothing, and the one thing that I loved more than anything just wasn't good enough until she died. And now, she was all I wanted. Sitting down on the dark wooden floors of the living room, I picked up Sparky and checked on his paws. They still looked pretty scorched. I needed to get this dog to a vet soon. I left a note for Max on the table and went to the village to get Sparky's feet checked out by a vet. Hopefully, there was one in the Onyx Valley village.

Walking through the town, I carried Sparky in my arms and looked through at all the small huts made of scrap metal. The town was like a giant, scrap-metal dump yard. Dwarves were around me left and right just enjoying their lives, working in the mines, and building go karts or whatever they desired. I envied them as they seemed so care free. They were so far from the war that they didn't have anything to worry about for now. After a while of searching, I found a village doctor that worked on animals as well as humans. I left Sparky with him and went searching for some clothes that fit Max. There was a lot of options since the Dwarves were all about Max's size. I found some stuff and headed back to the vet, but before I knew it, I was grabbed. A man's hand covered my mouth as I was dragged into the nearest alleyway. I panicked and tried to fight back, but the guy injected me with something that began to make me dizzy. Then I saw who it was. Brad Hart, the leader of the Pretty Boy crushers.

"Hurry. Tie him up, and throw him on the raptor," he said. "Qadir wants to see him right away."

Then everything went black.

CHAPTER FOURTEEN:

The twilight

Brad and his lackeys, Brendan and Keith, brought me into the castle of the Sanctuary, my old home, which Qadir had taken over a year ago. We entered the town just outside the castle walls. Everything looked so horrible. It used to be filled with energy and life, but what I saw was heart breaking. The people of the town looked so bitter. As I walked by, the people, who were out and about, either stared at me in shock or glared with hate. The town looked like a dump. It used to be so high class. The Sanctuary use to be like Beverly Hills but with more trees and not a tropical kind of look. Everything was super rich, and now, it was like an abandoned neighborhood you'd see in apocalyptic movies.

Looking at all the people was pretty depressing. They all looked so poverty-stricken. This made sense as Qadir loved to watch people suffer now that he was a closet Twilight creature. He wasn't one of those crazy soulless ones like the Twilight creatures that were at seaside. He had a soul the same way Ariel did. The twilight creatures with souls still looked like humans but deformed. My original plan before I decided to stay on the good side was to turn everyone in the Realms into a Twilight creature, so I would have control of the entire world and no one would mess with me—especially my father.

"Mason!"

My eyes turned to the man running right at us, the baker, Clark Hacher, Caroline's father. I felt my heart drop as I saw his face filled with worry. He must not know yet. I don't think anyone did. Everyone probably thought she was with me.

Brad immediately stopped Clark from getting any closer to me. "Get back to your shop, old man," he said and pushed Clark to the ground.

I tried to punch Brad for that, but Keith and Brendan held me back.

"Please. I just need to know if my daughter is okay," he pleaded on the ground with mud now all over his pants, not that it changed much as there was already dirt all over them. Many of the villagers were covered in dirt.

Brad chuckled and kicked him. Again, I tried to hurt Brad for it but was restrained. "Your daughter is dead because of him." He pointed at me.

Clark looked up at me in shock with tears filling his eyes. "Mason, please tell me he's lying."

I held back tears myself. I couldn't show weakness in front of Brad or his idiots. I just nodded and looked away from him.

Brad kicked him again. "Get out of here."

Clark shot up and punched Brad square in the face. "What happened to her?" Clark asked as Brad crashed to the muddy, stone ground.

I took a deep breath and looked at him. "Q-Qadir...he ripped her heart out."

His faced turned cold, and he glared at the castle, not even looking back at me one last time. He just went back to his bakery and slammed the door. I sighed just staring at the door, knowing that behind it was a broken man who just lost the only thing that mattered to him. Brad got back up, and we headed for the castle.

Bursting into the throne room, I looked around. Lexi was chained to the wall, which were made of some sort of crystal. It clearly had to be diamond, pure diamonds. Diamonds to the Sorcerers of Sonyin were like kryptonite for Superman. It weakened us, and our powers were useless if it was touching us. That's probably how Lexi hadn't been able to escape.

Qadir sat proudly on Matt's black wooden throne. It had golden trims and black velvet cushioning. I remember always putting bags filled with whatever random things Bridget and I could think of on the throne and waited for Matt to sit on them. He was never very observant, so he would always fall for it until one day he hired a throne watcher so that Bridget and I could no longer do that to him.

"Ah, Mason. Finally, you are here to join the party." Qadir smiled.

I just glared at him, keeping my mouth shut for now. I wanted to kill him so badly.

"Your birthday is tomorrow, is it not? I have been waiting for this," he said.

"If you know where I am twenty-four seven, why wait 'til now to take me?" I asked.

Qadir seemed surprised to be asked that question. "I guess it just made things more fun."

"So, this entire time, you knew where I was?"

Qadir nodded at my question.

"What game are you playing?" I questioned.

"It's not a game, Mason. This is life, and this is reality. My reality and hopefully yours," Qadir stated.

Looking at him skeptically, I sighed, "What are you talking about?"

"The world will soon be in complete darkness. No one can stop me. The older you get, the stronger the Twilight gets, and the more corrupted the world will be. That world will be the ideal world for us to live together," he rambled. "Eventually, it will be just you and me as I plan to kill everyone else off anyway."

I burst into laughter, "I would never ever live in a world like that especially with you."

Qadir just continued to smile. Without any warning, he socked me right in the stomach, and I crashed to my knees. Brad, Brendan, and Keith stepped a few feet away from me.

"Mason!" Lexi screamed.

Before I knew it, I was getting the beating of a life time. Lexi screamed and cried, begging Qadir to stop. I began to fight back, but he, being a god, made that almost impossible.

"Stop hurting him!" Lexi continued to beg.

Eventually, the beating stopped. My lip was torn open, blood poured from my face, and my stomach felt as if I had been kicked by a horse. Boy, did this bring back unwanted childhood memories.

Qadir went back to the throne and sat down. "Now, back to the point."

I lay there on the ground unable to even get up.

Being mortal really sucked.

"I need you to take your sister's magic," Qadir stated with a sadistic grin. He seemed to be enjoying himself, but if you looked closely, you could see the anger hidden in his twisted eyes. "Do it right now. I was going to wait until tomorrow when you were even stronger. However, I lost my patience with you."

"No! He can't take my magic," Lexi told Qadir. "He'll die. He can't control the force of light without his darkness to balance it out, and I really doubt you plan on giving him his powers back."

"If he dies, he is too weak to fulfill what I need, and I shouldn't waste my time on someone weak," Qadir said simply.

I sat up, feeling my head pounding, and wiped blood from my face. "I won't do it."

"You will or else..." Qadir glared then continued to smirk as he held up my element stone.

My eyes widened.

"I'll kill your sister."

"You wouldn't. She still has the light force," I sneered. "You can't kill her."

"Take her magic, or else I will. No matter what the consequences," Qadir said firmly.

"Please, Qadir, don't do this... He'll die," Lexi pleaded.

"I love him, Lexi," Qadir said as he gazed at my sister. "I would never do anything that would get him killed."

"Do you even know what you're doing?" I asked.

"I don't need to know," Qadir said, facing me again.

"Why is that?" I wondered.

"Because he knows. He told me everything I

needed to know," Qadir confessed. His face turned sincere then. "He told me how to live a happy life with you."

"You're so creepy. I don't want to be with you. I don't love you. I was just using you this entire time," I told him. My tone was harsh, and my voice a bit hoarse, but I didn't care. "I lied. I hate you. I only acted like I cared about you, so you would do whatever I wanted. So, have some pride, and get over me."

Qadir's expression turned cold. "So, you do not care that I am doing all of this for you? So, you can live in a world alone like you have always wanted?"

"I don't want to be alone especially if you are the only other person I'd have to talk to," I said. "Qadir, kill me. Hurt me. Just leave this world alone," I begged as my tone went from harsh to sad. "There's no point in this."

Qadir shot up in rage. "I will burn this world you love so dearly to the ground, kill everyone in it, and let you live just so you can walk in the ashes of your loved ones, knowing that it was your fault that they are all dead!"

I took a deep breath. How much pain did he want me to take? "I won't let you."

"You cannot stop me! You will never be able to protect the ones you love!" Qadir continued to yell in anger, and as he did, he transformed into his true form, the form I turned him into. He had glowing yellow eyes, and his skin turned pure black. His Twilight form—the Twilight form—was like a reflection of the soul. The further the soul went into the darkness, the more frightening the Twilight form would get. Qadir had one of the darkest souls, and soon, he wouldn't even have one. "Just look at Caroline. I killed her with ease. I kidnapped your sister and brother, and you never even came for them. You are no hero, Mason. Stop acting like you are."

He was right; who did I think I was? I couldn't save anyone. Caroline was dead because I couldn't save her. I looked away from Qadir, and a few tears slipped out. I was pathetic, useless, and worthless. I never could do anything right. I'm an idiot. I only ever made things worse. What was I thinking? I am no hero.

Qadir walked over to me and grabbed my face, digging his nails into my cheek. I winced in pain a bit as he wiped the tears off my face. "Just give up."

"Mason, do not listen to him," Lexi said. "You made mistakes. So what? Everyone does. You couldn't have saved Caroline, so don't let him make you think for one second that you could have because that will only fill you with regret."

"Shut her up," Qadir said to Brad.

Brad nodded and walked over to Lexi.

"Mason, please don't give up! Please don't. I need you. We all need yo—." Lexi cried.

Brad covered her mouth, leaving her words to a quiet mumble as she struggled to break out of his grip with her long wavy blonde hair all in her face. Lexi seemed to believe in me, even after she knew what I did, knowing I started this all. She believed in me regardless, and I couldn't let her down, right? But how could I stop Qadir? I couldn't ever take my magic back. This was hopeless.

"Since I don't need you anymore, I will just keep your sister," Qadir stated and released my face, scratching my cheek so badly that it bled as he let go.

"What?! No." I glared.

"She can be my new queen." Qadir smirked and

went over to Lexi.

I bolted up to attack him, but the stupid, goddamn Pretty Boy Crushers held me back.

"Qadir!" Emilia yelled as she ran in. "There's a mob outside. They're demanding your head."

Qadir stopped in his tracks and looked at Emilia. "Have the guards slaughter them all," he ordered.

Emilia nodded and ran off.

"Now, where...where did she go?!"

I shot my gaze over to Qadir. I was too distracted by Emilia that I didn't notice Lexi had escaped, and Pie was standing where she used to be, smirking like an idiot. He seemed so proud to pull a fast one like that on his father. I laughed a bit from the relief. I didn't want to know what that bastard had planned for her.

"Hi, Daddy," Pie said as he continued to give Qadir a bright smug smirk.

Qadir glared coldly at his son. "Pippin."

I snorted and held back a laugh. His real name was Pippin. *Wow.*

Bridget walked in, laughing so hard. "I am sorry. I was going to make a dramatic entrance and all like you said, but then I heard your name, and I just couldn't take it."

Qadir probably had several wives in his life, which was over 1,000 years. I don't know who Pie's mother was, but he looked nothing like Qadir. The only wife of Qadir I had ever meet was Susalea who also looked nothing like Pie and would never name her child Pippin. Who knew how old Pie was? I know he's not a mortal or a demigod. But that meant if Qadir died, Pie would become the new god of Mischief, which would be fitting for him.

Bridget ran over to me before Qadir could stop

her. Brad stepped up and tried to kill her.

"Seriously Brad?" Bridget glared and kicked him hard in the stomach.

He went tumbling to the ground, and she smashed his head hard on the ground, knocking him out. Brendan and Keith dropped me and began to fight her too, but they got their butts kicked. Pie distracted Qadir by using his weird mischievous powers to surround Qadir in an invisible box, making him look like a mime.

"Mason, go! Griffin and Lexi are waiting for you outside!" Pie yelled.

Emilia grabbed me before I could run. "You aren't going anywhere."

Bridget stopped and glared at Emilia after she finished off Brendan and Keith. Those guys were truly pathetic. Also, Bridget was a skilled fighter, and they didn't stand a chance. "Let him go Emilia, or I will rip your perky little heart out," Bridget warned her, wearing her guardian of the Realms uniform.

So was Pie, but Pie's was different than ours. Instead of one color and a silver trimming, he was like a walking rainbow. I could never ever take this guy seriously. Bridget held up her scythe, giving Emilia the look of murder.

Emilia sighed, "Screw it. I hated working for this guy anyway." She dropped me then vanished.

I got back up on my feet. I was so lucky that my wounds healed quicker than normal people, or I would be screwed right now.

"We gotta go guys," Pie said as he walked over to us. "My father could break out any moment."

"All right, come on," I said and ran off toward the hall Bridget entered from. I tried not to limp, but it was hard not to. My leg hurt like hell, and I was still not over the beating I had gotten from Qadir.

Bridget and Pie followed me out to the nearest balcony that overlooked the town from the castle. There was fire everywhere, and soldiers fought civilians. I never thought the people of the Realms ever would gain the guts to fight back against Qadir. This was truly amazing.

"It's awesome, isn't it?" Griffin said as he walked up to me. Lexi followed closely behind. "Caroline's dad started it all."

I looked at him with a smile. "Really?"

"Yeah, and there's now rebellion all over the Realms." Griffin smiled. "They're fighting back, and they aren't afraid anymore."

"Guys!" Lexi panicked. "The Twilight. He sent out the Twilight!"

"What are we going to do?!" Bridget asked in fear.

Watching the people struggle so much for freedom, knowing that this rebellion against Qadir started because of Caroline, I knew I had to stop Qadir from hurting them. I had to take Qadir's power from him. I had to prove I was not weak and that he was wrong. I am strong.

I looked over at Bridget. "I know how to stop it."

"I'm not killing you if that's what you're suggesting," Lexi remarked.

I sighed, "No, Lexi. I have to take my power back," I told them and began to walk down the stairs that led to the courtyard where the Twilight was heading and where the people were fighting.

"Mason, no!" Lexi yelled and ran after me. Everyone else followed. "You'll lose yourself. It will consume you."

I didn't stop. I couldn't waste any time. "Lexi, I'm strong and no longer afraid. Fear is what drove me down. Now, just trust me," I said and went faster.

I entered the courtyard and ran past the fight. Griffin, Bridget, and Pie began to help the people the best they can. I went over to the gates where the Twilight was coming from. I could see them coming toward us at a fast pace. The golden gate was the only thing in their way from killing everyone—well, the gate and me. I gazed back at the castle one last time and saw Qadir watching me. I gave him a little smirk, turned back to the Twilight, and ran at them. I heard

Qadir yell in rage behind me, but I didn't stop. I ran faster and faster until the Twilight and I collided. Before I knew it, I jerked my head back, standing firmly as I absorbed the power of the Twilight, the power of corruption.

Everything went black, but I could feel myself absorb it. It felt like a bunch of knives piercing my body, and the pain was unbearable. Suddenly, I dropped as the pain left me, and I knew at that moment I had succeeded and that everything was about to change.

CHAPTER FIFTEEN:

Pain

The battle came to an immediate stop as everyone saw what had happened. I faced them. They all stared at me in shock. Qadir then appeared before the crowd. I just smirked at him.

"You haven't won yet." Qadir glared. "The Twilight will drive you mad."

"Not this time. I'm not afraid of myself anymore or anything," I said with power in my voice, standing tall, so he knew I would not be messed with. "The Realms will be free!"

The people cheered as Qadir's soldiers waited for Qadir's words. Lexi walked up to me and stood by my side. Bridget, Griffin, and Pie followed her and did the same. Qadir was no longer in his Twilight form. It must've went back into hiding after I took the Twilight back. He continued to sneer at me. He knew he could no longer hurt me. I was no longer some weak mortal he could push around as all gods do.

I stood tall and looked toward the soldiers who were still frozen from shock. I knew what they were thinking. They were thinking that I was going to kill them all right there with the Twilight. I could very well set them loose on all of them and kill them all, but I knew if I did, the citizens of the Sanctuary would be afraid of me.

"Any men who want to join us stay. But if you choose to fight for Qadir, then leave now or die," I said loudly so everyone could hear.

"Don't let him scare you! Kill everyone!" Qadir yelled at his soldiers.

None of them moved until a minute later. Almost half of them ran off into the woods, and a few dropped their weapons to the ground. That's when everyone in the crowd raised a fist and shouted. "Long Live The Realms!"

I smiled brightly and looked at Qadir smugly.

"You haven't won just yet, Mason. The game isn't over," Qadir said and vanished into a large green cloud of smoke that swirled around him.

Everyone cheered and rejoiced. They were free. However, Qadir would come back. I had to eliminate him for good, which meant I had to go find Kule Palace and free the Sonyin Sorcerers. Only Grace, the goddess of Wisdom, could kill him, or at least, her element stone. If she gave us that or agreed to use it, we could kill him, and the Realms would truly be free. But first, I assumed that everyone wanted to celebrate. I should probably send word to Matt. Oh, and send someone to get Sparky and Max. I hoped they were okay.

Eventually, everyone gathered in the ballroom in the castle. We were able to find where Qadir was hiding all the food, and the citizens had full stomachs again in a long time. That was a happy thought.

"Nice work," Matt said as he walked over to me.

I was standing in the corner away from the large crowd since I wasn't too fond of large crowds. "Thanks, but it's not over yet," I told him.

"I know it's not, but you still did well for an idiot," Matt said.

I shot a glare at him.

"So where were you all those months?"

"Onyx Valley. I have a secret house there," I confessed.

"How did you manage that?" he asked.

"It's a secret," I said.

He sighed, "All right...so where's Caroline?"

I looked at him confused. Did he really not know? "She's gone."

"What do you mean gone?" Matt questioned.

"She died..." I told him. "I buried her and ran off for months because I didn't want to deal with life, knowing she wouldn't be around anymore."

"I am sorry to hear that," he said. "I know what it's like to lose someone."

"Do you?" I questioned.

"Yes, although the one I lost has returned to me." Matt then looked over at Max who was in the corner playing with Sparky.

I smiled at the sight. It was so heartwarming. I was glad they got back safely though I kind of wanted to know how they got back.

"Did Max tell you what happened to him?" I asked Matt. If Max told him,

Matt should be furious with me. So, I assume he didn't, but I just wanted to make sure.

"He said Qadir captured him and locked him up

deep under the castle of the Sanctuary," Matt told me.

"Oh," I muttered.

"He also told me that Qadir brought him to you. Thanks for taking care of him, He said you helped him get all the tangles out of his hair and gave him clean clothes. You're a good big brother." He smiled.

If only he knew what I did, then he wouldn't be saying that. "Anyway, uh, I have to go," I said quickly to avoid the topic and walked over to Max.

He looked up at me as he sat there petting Sparky. "You know if you're getting kidnapped, at least, write a note first," he joked with a small little grin.

"Ha. Ha. You're hilarious," I said sarcastically and sat next to him. "So, I see you got a good pair of clothes that fit you."

"Yeah," Max said.

Instead of the dirty ripped-up clothes he was wearing when I first found him, he was wearing a gray, long-sleeved shirt with a cartoon bunny on it. He had a thing for bunnies, and he really loved them. He also wore black denim shorts that went down to his knees and old, black sneakers that were familiar to me. They were mine from when I was his age. He must've found my old clothes and gave them to Max. Matt adopted me when I was about ten, so he had my old clothes lying around here somewhere. I wore black all the time when I was a kid, so most of my clothes were black. Now, I wore mostly blue and other colors. The way I dressed in Leadville was weird. I never thought I would wear band t-shirts and a white vans jacket all the time. I usually wore button downed shirts with the sleeves rolled up, and my pants were black jeans almost always. Sometimes, I would wear normal blue jeans, but I was really into black jeans. Skinny jeans but not too tight, so my downtown wasn't in any pain.

Sparky was cuddling on Max's lap, snoozing. I smiled at him. "He really likes you."

Max looked down at Sparky too and smiled his dorky little smile. He had a gap in between his teeth, so his smile was so goofy but adorable. "Yeah, I really like him too."

I sighed a bit. This was going to be hard, but I never took proper care of Sparky, and it seemed like Max really cared about him. So, I figured might as well. "You want him?"

Max face beamed as he looked up at me in excitement. "Really?"

"Yeah, I'm always so busy and usually neglect the poor thing," I explained. "Also, you can think of it as a way of me saying I'm sorry for what I have done."

Max kept the bright smile on his face. "Thank you, Mason. This is great."

"You're welcome, kid," I said.

"Hey, Max," Cano said as she kneeled down in front of us. "It's getting late. You should head to bed."

"But Dad said I could stay up tonight." He pouted.

Cano's dark, black hair was tied back in a ponytail as usual, and her skin was tanner than normal, probably because she spent so much time outside in the rebellion. Her eyes were still like dazzling purple gems. To me, they were her only good quality. Okay, I'm kidding. She was a very beautiful woman, but I hated her personality. Cano and I hated each other, and I am sure it was going to forever be that way.

"Well, your dad lied. Now, go," Cano said and pointed to the doors.

Max stood up. Suddenly, my head filled with

unbearable pain. I screamed out from the pain and held the sides of my head. Everyone began to crowd me with worry. I began to get dizzy, and the pain wasn't helping my sight very well either. All my senses were beginning to dull.

"Get help!" Someone yelled.

Good luck beating me now. Qadir's stupid voice echoed in my head, and I sneered.

"Can't you heal him, Lexi?" Bridget asked as I looked up at her. She looked frightened, and so did Lexi and Griffin.

"Get him to the infirmary," Susalea said as she pushed through the crowd. "Matt, help me lift him up."

Matt came over, picked me up, and threw me over his shoulder. I let out another cry of pain, and of course, Matt had to comment. "Stop being a baby, ya pansy."

I wanted to die. The pain was too much. My brain literally felt like it was about to explode, and that wasn't a good sign obviously. I knew I was going to be okay because the only thing that could kill me was Lexi. If my head really did explode, I would still be alive. Thanks to the wonderful thing called magic, eventually my head would just magically appear again like it had never exploded in the first place. I guess that was a beauty about being a god though I always felt like being a god was like cheating in life. I'd never die, not unless my sister hated me enough to kill me, which she didn't as far as I was concerned. I could do anything I wanted and look however I wanted.

Being born to become the cruelest and most powerful god in existence wasn't fun at all. Don't get me wrong. Being able to control someone just by talking was pretty cool. I could also turn people into raging monsters that would do whatever I say. But the problem was I never wanted any of it. Taking this power wasn't my choice. My father just insisted and forced me to, and when I did, I was just being the obedient little boy I always had to be. I had no idea what it would do to me. I was a monster, a murder, and just down right horrible. My father was an idiot though. He should've known that I wouldn't do what he said forever. I hated him so much. Everything I became was his fault. He was the one person that truly scared me, and that wasn't something I was happy about. I felt weak and pathetic around him, so in a way, I did everything to try to prove to him I wouldn't be messed with. But as usual, that blew up in my face like everything always does.

  I suppose I should get over it and just move on. I should just forget about all the times my father would beat me senseless or the time he tried to drown me, knowing that I wouldn't die. He just kept me under the water until I passed out. I should also just forget about the time he left me in a room with the worst dead souls he had locked away. His reasoning for that was that if I can handle them, I can handle anyone. To this day, I have nightmares about the things they said and did. But no one knew what I had been through during my childhood, and I didn't plan on telling anyone. I had to act as if nothing happened because if I did, people would tell me I was being overly dramatic—especially since I'm a boy. Boys aren't allowed to have feelings without being insulted, which was absolutely ridiculous. However, I never really cared what anyone thought of me most of the time.

  "Mason, just breathe. It will be okay," Max said calmly as he sat beside my bed, holding my hand.

"What's wrong with him?" Cano asked Susalea who was checking my eyes.

Cano stood a few feet away from the bed, and Matt sat in a chair beside her, watching me. Practically, everyone was in the room, Ambriel, Lexi, Bridget, Griffin, even Pie, and that meant he was missing out on the dessert table. Susalea sighed as I tried to keep in my cries of pain. I was doing pretty well, but every now and then, I'd let out a quiet scream. I tried to make it stop, but none of my magic was working.

"I don't know what's wrong with him," Susalea said. "Mason, stop using your powers. It will only drain you."

"It was Qadir!" I yelled as my head raged with agony even more.

"We figured that. We want to know what he did to cause you such pain that can't be reversed," Lexi remarked. "Ambriel, can you do something?"

"Oh, please, when could Ambriel do anything?" Griffin commented.

"Hey!" Ambriel glared at him with her wings hidden again. Instead of the purple dress I saw her in before, she wore a long white dress. She was pretty as always.

"Leave her alone, Griffin," I told him and took a deep breath.

"Just saying she's a horrible guardian angel," Griffin sighed.

Lexi smacked him on the arm.

"He's right. I am horrible." Ambriel frowned, ran over to me, and hugged me tightly. "I'm sorry. I'm sorry. I am so sorry," she said over and over as she swayed me in her arms that I couldn't breathe.

"Ambriel," I mumbled. "Ambriel, it's okay. Let me

go."

She didn't let go for another thirty seconds, but eventually, she stopped saying sorry and went back over to Bridget.

"All right. How are we going to reverse this stupid spell?" Lexi asked.

"What if it's not even a spell?" Griffin questioned.

"Is it a doughnut? Sorry, That was stupid. I'm just really hungry," Pie commented.

"G-Go eat, Pie. I'll be okay," I told him.

Pie didn't hesitate to run out of the room to go stuff his face, which I figured he would do.

"I'll go look up what I can do, Mason. Don't move from this room," Susalea ordered and left.

"You're going to be okay, right?" Max asked timidly.

I looked at him the best I could though my vision was still a bit blurry. Giving him a smile, I ruffled his hair a bit. "Yeah, I'll be fine."

"What are we going to do?" Griffin asked. "Qadir will kill everyone now."

"Lexi can stop him. She's stronger than Mason," Cano said.

"I can't fight Qadir, and I can't kill him. Not without Grace," Lexi said.

"Then get her. Ask her to help," I told her. "I can come with you."

"No, you can't. You need to rest," Bridget stated flatly. "Lexi, Griffin, and I will go."

"I have to go. Only I can lift the force field from Kule Palace." I pointed out and took a deep breath, trying not to scream again. I shot up and almost banged my head into the wall. It hurt that bad. I stopped myself before I did because that would've just made it worse. The pain was usually constant, but sometimes, the pain would pause for a moment, and I would feel relief in my head. Then a minute or two later, it would come back. I hated Qadir so much.

"I can do it, Mason. Just trust me. And if I can't, I'll come and get you," Lexi said. "We can't wait. If we wait, he will kill everyone."

"He doesn't have the Twilight anymore." I pointed out and held my head again.

"So? He's a god, and he can still kill people easily," Lexi argued. "I'm going without you. You just have to trust that I'll be okay." With that, she walked out of the room.

Griffin looked at me. "I will keep her safe..." he promised and followed her.

I turned to Bridget. "Don't let them go without me," I begged her.

She sighed and shrugged. "I can't stop them now, but I'll go and keep them company to make sure they don't get into too much trouble."

"Take Pie with you. He's strong," I said.

She nodded. "Will do." Bridget smiled and left as well.

I sighed and looked at Matt a bit worried. "She's going to be okay, right?"

Matt nodded. "Yeah, it's Lexi. She's not someone anyone should mess with. She'd kick Qadir's ass easily."

"Then why hasn't she before?" I questioned.

"You never gave her the chance to," Cano cut in.

I glared at Cano. "Shut up."

"She's right. You're too protective of Lexi sometimes. You got to let her fight too. She has every right to," Matt said.

"Whatever," I sighed and lay back down, letting out a small cry from the pain.

Max gasped, "I know what's wrong with you!" he said ecstatically.

Everyone immediately looked at him, including me.

"I have to go find Susalea!" he yelled and ran out the door.

"Max!" Cano shouted and ran after him.

Hopefully, Max really did know what was wrong with me.

CHAPTER SIXTEEN:

The fall

Max explained to me what he figured was wrong with me. He got Susalea, and she confirmed what was wrong. It was a form of magic as suspected. It wasn't Qadir's magic though; it was known as death magic— my father's magic. I put it together when Max told me. I realized what this meant. Alash was working with Qadir. he must've been the *he* Qadir was talking about. Either way, the only way to reverse the magic put on me was to use life magic. The great thing about the elements of Sonyin sorcerers is that normal sorcerers can use the elements. It's just not as powerful as our magic. The only force that no mere mortal can mimic was Lexi's and mine. Hopefully, we could find a life sorcerer strong enough to heal me.

My head just got worse and worse as they pain seemed to never end. "So, what are we going to do?" I asked painfully.

"We need to get help. Obviously," Max said. "But I don't know anyone strong enough to break magic this strong."

I sighed with pain still shooting through my mind.

"What about the Druids?" Matt asked.

"You freed them?" I questioned.

"No, Qadir still has them," Cano said. "This means they aren't an option."

"We could sneak Mason in or sneak one of them out," Matt suggested.

"Good idea," I said sarcastically.

"It's actually not bad," Susalea commented.

I rolled my eyes, which oddly made my head hurt more. Screw Qadir for making my sass painful.

"It will be hard but—" Susalea was cut off by Zack, the troll.

"Qadir. He's coming. He's coming to finish us off," he warned us. He was tired and out of breath. Clearly, he was in a hurry.

"How do you know?" Matt asked, worried.

"Prince Mason shouldn't see this, but come with me," he said, wiping a booger from his nose.

"I have to see his warning," I argued.

"Can you even see?" Cano asked.

"Yes, Cano. The message was from Qadir. I have to see it," I stated. "He most likely directed it toward me anyway."

"He did, Prince Mason, and that is why my brothers and I have decided that it's best you didn't see," Zack stated. He talked pretty formally for a troll.

"I am seeing it," I stated and got on my feet. The ground was cold at first, but eventually, it warmed up beneath my feet. I stumbled a bit as I headed for the door.

Matt was right next to me and took my arm, trying to make sure I didn't fall. "Careful. You don't want to hurt that pretty little face of yours," he teased.

I shot a glare at him and jerked my arm from his grip. Surprisingly, I strutted down the hall with no problem. I was determined to show him I could stand on my own. I headed for the courtyard with Matt, Max, and Cano following me. Going outside, I saw Qadir's warning. I never thought he'd stoop so low it would be this horrifying. I guess I made him this way.

On the ground only a few feet away from me was Caroline's corpse lying in the ground. It smelled repulsive that everyone covered their noses and mouths instantly. Her rotting corpse lay in a pool of blood as the dead bodies of nine deer hung from the trees by their legs with the names of everyone I loved carved into the sides of the innocent animals. Bridget, Griffin, Matt, Lexi, Max, Cano, Pie, Ambriel, and even Sparky. My stomach grew sick. I was seriously going to vomit. I dropped to my knees and tried to breathe, but the sight was so horrifying I lost my breath.

"Get rid of this quickly," Matt ordered the guards at the door.

I didn't want to, but I began to sob as I looked at Caroline's dead body lying there. I didn't want to play this game anymore. The guards went over to the trees and began to attempt to take the deer down, but they went flying right when they did and laughter echoed around us, his laughter—Qadir's twisted laughter.

Cano quickly took Max inside the castle. Matt drew his sword immediately, and the troll brothers, Zack, Phillip, and Jordane, prepared to guard Matt and me since the guards were probably dead. My head began to hurt more, and I began to scream from the pain. I dropped to the ground as it got worse and more unbearable than ever before. Tears still streamed down my face. I landed in the pool of blood next to Caroline's corpse.

"Get out of here, Qadir!" Matt yelled.

My screaming grew silent. I was in too much pain to even scream anymore. I just lay there in pain, trying to refrain from vomiting because of the smell. I could no longer hear or see anything. I could feel the warm blood on my skin. I tried to imagine it was something else, but I couldn't get the image of blood out of my head. What made it all worse was that a quiet whisper rang through my mind, telling me I should just get used to the feeling of blood on my hands. It was the road I was heading down. I wouldn't let myself get to that point. This time, the Twilight won't win. The pain in my head faded suddenly after I felt a gentle touch on my forehead. I gasped with relief as my vision began to return. To my surprise, kneeling above me was my mother, Melanie. She was smiling down at me with her gentle face. Something about her just made everything around me peaceful.

My mother had the same long, sunshine-blonde, wavy hair, which was longer hair than Lexi's. Her eyes were green like spring grass, and her skin was sun-kissed ivory. Lexi looked a lot like her. My mother was a goddess, so of course, she was wearing a pure-white dress with long see-through sleeves. She wore a crown of leaves, and yellow daffodils covered the collar of her white dress. Those were her favorite flowers. She said they reminded her of the sun.

"Are you okay?" she asked with a calming voice. I would know her voice anywhere.

I nodded and sat up, but immediately, tumbled back to the ground.

Sighing, Matt kneeled down and picked me up, carrying me inside.

I didn't want to seem weak around him. I gazed back at what Qadir did in the courtyard. It sickened me to see it, yet at the same time, I couldn't look away. Qadir was planning to kill everyone I loved, so I had no one but him to care for. What a demented thought. He should realize that doing so would just make me hate him. He was driven by his obsession for something he could never have. Griffin was out at the courtyard with Bridget, Pie, and Lexi. As I entered the hall, I could see them through the window. Lexi began to cry as Bridget hugged her to comfort her. I'm sure Lexi and everyone else wished that we didn't have to deal with another day of pain. I couldn't help but feel guilty because I forced them into this. I forced them into my war.

That's when I decided that I had to fight Qadir on my own and that no one else was allowed to get hurt. Especially The ones I loved. Maybe that's what Qadir wanted, but whether he wanted it or not, I refused to let him take anyone else from me.

It was time to destroy Qadir for good.

It was time Caroline was avenged.

It had been a few hours or so after I showered, I fell asleep in my old room. The walls painted a dark gray-blue color, and the floors were mahogany like most of the castle floors. A crystal chandelier draped down from the ceiling, lighting up the entire room. My desk was covered in random junk I threw on there like papers or cool rocks I'd find when I was out exploring the Realms, pens, and so much more. I needed to organize this place. Surprisingly, Qadir hasn't moved anything when he took over the Sanctuary. I'm sure he came in here, probably smelled my pillows and hugged my clothes like the freak he was. It was nice to finally be able to relax for a bit with no pain in my mind aside from my worries.

I knew I had to get up soon, so I could get Grace's element stone of wisdom to kill Qadir. No one would miss him, so I'm sure she wouldn't mind handing it over. I wasn't sure if Lexi got it or not, but she did get the gods free, which I didn't think she'd manage especially so fast. I underestimated Lexi a lot. The element stone would be hard to use on Qadir as it's not just something where you cast a spell, and boom, he's dead. The element stone was a celestial weapon. It turned into whatever you wanted to fight with and could kill a mortal with just a scratch, but to kill a god, you had to hit them right in their heart. I was going to have to find a way to get close to Qadir without him pulling me away. The bright side was that Qadir couldn't kill me without Lexi's element stone. I really doubt he had hers too. He found mine, so I guess hiding it in the seventies was a bad idea. He could kill Lexi if he wanted to. I couldn't let that happen.

I sat up stretching when I was grabbed abruptly and dragged out of bed. "Whoa, Bridget. What's going on?" I asked as she pulled me out of my room and down the hall. What could possibly be going on now?

We entered the dining hall. Right when we walked in, everyone jumped out yelling happy birthday at the top of their lungs. I stood there awkwardly. I forgot it was my birthday. Lexi, Max, Griffin, Matt, Pie, and Cano were all gathered around the large, glass table that had a large rainbow cake with the words

"HAPPY BIRTHDAY PRINCESS" on it with a small pile of presents next to the cake.

I chuckled, "Nice cake."

"I know it's been a rough day for you, but we thought we'd at least celebrate your birth." Bridget smiled.

"Thanks." I smiled at everyone and walked over to them. "So, whose idea was it to write happy birthday princess on the cake?"

"Mine." Griffin smirked.

"Thanks, man. Come here. I want to hug you," I said.

Griffin chuckled, "No way. You're going to hit me or something."

I quickly grabbed him and shoved him face first into the cake. I wasn't a fan of cake anyway, so I didn't plan on eating it.

Lexi laughed and so did most everyone.

Only Pie didn't laugh. He just gasped, "I worked hard on that cake!" Pie cried.

Griffin lifted his head up with cake all over him. I laughed, but before I could react, I got a face full of cake. "That's a good look on you," he laughed.

Taking a moment, I wiped the cake off my face and attempted to throw another piece of cake at Griffin, but before I knew it, Lexi dumped the entire cake on my head. I let out a small scream. The room filled with laughter.

"Happy nineteenth birthday!" Lexi shouted and smiled. "I love you," she laughed.

"I'm so glad I spent hours cooking over a hot oven for this," Pie sassed.

"Dude, you just bought a cake from Clark," Griffin said.

"Don't tell him that!" Pie yelled.

"I am going to go shower. Again," I said.

"No, open your presents first," Max cut in, handing me a wrapped box.

I sighed and took the box, ripping the wrapping off. I opened the small box, and there was a necklace with a white stone attached to it. I picked it up and looked at it, which was a miniature warp stone.

"I made it myself." Max smiled. "It's a warp stone that you can carry with you. It works really well, but you have to let it recharge for five minutes after every use."

"Thanks, Max, this is really cool and actually very useful." I smiled at him. Normally, people would just get me random junk for my birthday, but this was actually valuable. I put it back in the box and set it on the table. "Can I open the rest later? I really want this cake out of my hair."

"Fine, but hurry," Bridget told me.

I quickly ran off after that, going to my room to clean myself off. I was nineteen years old now, which meant the Twilight that I now had control over was stronger than ever before. The Twilight creatures could no longer die by a mortal blade. It had to be killed by a light weapon. A weapon of Lexi's creation. What an unfair advantage I had. There had to be a way to stop me other than just Lexi's light magic. I planned to do research on this to discover more stuff about my species. Sitting in the castle garden, I was lost in thought. I began to feel like maybe my mother was just an illusion. I hadn't seen her ever since what happened in the courtyard.

"Hey," Griffin said as he sat next to me.

"Hi," I sighed.

"You okay?" he asked.

"I don't know anymore," I confessed. "I just want this to be over."

"Everyone does, but Lexi got the wisdom element stone, so we should be ready for battle," Griffin told me.

"About that...I think I should go fight Qadir alone."

"What? No, you can't do it alone," he argued.

"Griffin, you have to understand. I can't lose anyone else," I began to explain. "He will not hesitate to kill you or anyone we care about."

"We still need to stick by each other!" he yelled. Griffin was always passionate about these kinds of things.

"You saw what he did. You saw her d—" I stopped and took a deep breath. It still hurt even after all the months of trying to get over her. "Dead. Caroline's dead because of him and because I couldn't protect her. When I fight Qadir, I can't be worrying if any of you are hurt or dead."

"You don't have to worry about us," Griffin argued. "We can take care of ourselves."

"That won't stop me from worrying," I sighed.

Griffin stayed quiet after that, and we just sat there for a while.

After a few minutes, Griffin finally spoke up again, "I had the guards bury Caroline for you, so you didn't have to again."

"Oh... Thanks," I mumbled. "Where did you bury her?"

"In that meadow just outside the castle where you two always used to go. I buried her under a tree and marked it with a headstone. I told her dad too, so he could visit," Griffin said.

I choked up a bit but kept my tears hidden. A heart-wrenching feeling filling me like it always did when I was forced to speak about her. Hopefully one day, I could talk about her without getting so distraught inside. That took time though. You'd think after a few months, I'd be better, but the pain made it feel as if she died yesterday. I knew I'd never be able to love again. She was the only one I could see myself with.

"Thank you," I said quietly.

"She was the reason you disappeared for months, right?" he asked.

I nodded. "Yes."

"I wish I could've stopped him... I was there. I watched him attack her. before I could do anything, he knocked me out cold," Griffin said sincerely. "I'm so sorry."

I bit my lip as he continued to talk. I really hated this conversation. I put my hand on his shoulder and looked at him in the eyes. "Griffin, you have nothing to be sorry for."

"I just want everything to be okay, you know? And they can't be okay if you aren't okay too. Because she's no longer with us, I'm worried you never will be," he confessed.

"Look. I'm going to be okay, so don't worry about me," I told him. "Focus on you. Sometimes, you forget to do that."

Griffin sighed, "That's ironic coming from you."

"It is?"

"All you do is worry about us. You don't care if you die or not as long as everyone else is okay," he said. "You gotta let others take care of you too, Mason.

It can't just be one-sided."

"I don't really need anyone to take care of me," I said. "I never have."

"You always have," he corrected me.

"No," I objected.

"You always have needed someone to take care of you. You just never let them," Griffin said.

"Whatever you say, man," I sighed.

"So...here." Griffin handed me a stone, which was white and shaped like a diamond. "Grace's element stone, the wisdom stone."

I took it and smiled a bit at Griffin. "Thanks."

"Go kill the bastard before he gets here with his army. No one else needs to die." Griffin smiled back sadly.

"I will go now. Just keep Bridget and Lexi here. Don't let them follow me," I told him.

"I'll try, but I don't make any promises," he said.

"Griffin, you have to keep them away, like, no exceptions," I said firmly. "I can't risk them getting hurt."

Griffin nodded with understanding. "Okay, they won't come near the fight."

"Is Qadir taking residence in his old castle now?"

"That's what Susalea said. She had a few members of the rebellion out looking for him," Griffin said.

"Then that's where I will head." I stated and stood up.

"Be careful. He's hard to kill," he told me and stood up as well.

"I will. Keep the Sanctuary safe while I'm gone. You never know what Qadir has planned," I said and shoved the stone in my pocket, heading toward the castle gates.

I made my way toward Sariah, one of the 13 kingdoms in the Realms controlled by Qadir. He was one of the few gods who didn't let a mortal take care of the kingdom for him. I rode a horse through the Ancient Woods, my mother's kingdom. I had to cross through her kingdom to get to Sariah. It was so peaceful and quiet, but I still kept my guard up. Who knows what was hunting me down? Qadir, his men, or even the Sonyin sorcerers could be after me right now. I'm certain some want revenge for being locked up for a year.

Making my way down the dirt path, I let out a sigh, petting my horse's mane. Fear may have been my enemy, but I was so afraid to face Qadir. However, if I didn't, no one else would. I was going to stop a war before it started, so no one had to die fighting for me. Especially innocent men and women who have nothing to do with it. The Realms only had a million or so people living throughout the entire kingdom, and we didn't need to lose them. I zoned out a bit as my horse and I continued down the path. I had so many different things on my mind, so I didn't notice when a skeleton of a wolf came charging at me, causing my horse to run away as fast as it could and me to crash to the ground. I was so tired of being attacked over and over.

I shot up on my feet, preparing to fight the wolf, but I froze when I saw my father, Alash, standing next to it. His face was stern. I really hated how much I looked like him. We had the same hair color and the exact same eye color, except mine were just a bit lighter. We had the same nose, and most of my facial features were the same. He was a lot tougher looking than me though. I didn't come off as violent or threatening, but he did. It repelled off of him. Everything about him made me uneasy. I honestly wanted to hide just being in his presence.

"The Sonyin sorcerers want you dead," he told me. His voice was still frightening as always. It was deep, and every time I heard him speak, I only wanted to claw my own throat out or smash my head into a wall.

"I figured," I mumbled.

"Stop mumbling. No one can understand you when you mumble," he scolded me, raising his voice.

I nodded nervously, so he knew I understood him. I tensed up and tried my hardest to stand straight, not making any movement just in case I upset him.

"I have never been so disappointed in you. You're a disgrace," he spat. "I truly hate you. Why was I given such a weak child? I didn't raise you to be this pathetic."

I stayed quiet, listening to his hateful words.

He paced around me, getting closer and closer as he walked. "Do you realize how worthless you are? I tried so hard to make you into something useful, but you couldn't live up to the standards because you are stupid. You're an idiot. No one loves you, and you managed to kill the only one who did."

My eyes began to twitch, and my breathing sped up. I felt a knot in my stomach as I stood there with my father only a foot away from my face.

"Do I need to teach you another lesson?!" he shouted with pure rage and hate.

I flinched instantly and stumbled back a bit.

"You're a coward," he sneered.

I felt a sharp pain in my arm and realized I was clawing at my skin. It was so bad that I broke skin.

When I saw blood, I immediately stopped. His eyes shifted to my arm, and he slapped me across the face.

"Alash!" a loud voice boomed behind him. It was my mother. I almost cried. "Get away from my son," She ordered him.

My father grabbed the back of my head by my hair and made me face my mother. "You mean our shit of a son?"

She glared at him. I've never seen her so pissed off. Before I knew it, Alash was wrapped up in a bunch of vines, and he was forced to release me. As soon as he did, I ran from him and went over to my mother.

Alash was filled with rage and instantly turned into a raven, causing the vines to fall to the ground. He flew off.

My mother pulled me into a big hug, holding me close. "I am so sorry for what he has said to you."

I wasn't much of a hugger, but since I rarely ever got to hug my mom, I hugged her back. "Thank you for getting him away from me," I said.

"I wish I got him away from you when you were a baby, then maybe things would be different," she spoke. Animals began to gather around us. It was odd, but I guess life naturally found its way to her. "You should get going. Qadir has already sent out his army. I sent my own army of high elves after them, but the fighting will only be prevented if you exterminate Qadir." She let me go from her hug.

"He doesn't have Lexi's element stone, so I shouldn't be afraid, right?" I asked her.

"You have nothing to fear but the fear that you aren't strong enough." She smiled. "Take the warpstone that Max gave you. It is your fastest way to Sariah," she informed me and made the white stone necklace appear around my neck.

"Goodbye, mother," I said and gripped onto the small warpstone around my neck, but before I teleported away, I was tackled hugged by Pie.

"Mason!" he shouted as we both struggled to stay on our feet from his hug.

"Pie!" I yelled in annoyance.

"I've been following you for quite some time now. Finally caught up to ya. Sorry about the hug. I got excited when I realized I found you," he explained himself as he released me from his hug. "I wanted to help you. Griffin said you wouldn't let him, Bridget, or Lexi. So, I figured I'd come."

I turned to look at my mother, but she was gone. I just looked back at Pie and sighed, "You came to help me kill your father?"

"You're really going to kill him?" he asked with a sad look on his face.

"I don't know what else to do, Pie," I told him and began walking down the path.

"He wasn't always bad. He was one of my heroes when I was younger," Pie said. "One day, he just changed like someone flipped a switch and suddenly made him psychotic."

That person was me was what I wanted to tell him. But how could I tell one of my best friends that his father supposedly fell in love with me? And I turned his father into a Twilight creature because I needed a god on my side that was evil and would let me boss him around?

"I'm sorry," I muttered, gazing at the ground, with guilt filling me.

"I really don't want him to die," Pie confessed to me. "So, Mason, when you fight my dad, all I ask is that you try to find a way to spare his life."

"I'll try," I promised him. "Now, come on," I said and held my hand out to him. "Let's save the Realms."

Pie took my hand, and I grasped the warpstone tightly in my hand and thought of Qadir's castle. Before I knew it, I was there in the courtyard of his castle. It was vacant. He probably sent every guard he had to go fight and slaughter everyone in the Sanctuary. I couldn't waste any more time. I darted inside, hoping that maybe he was there waiting for me.

Entering the ballroom, I scoped around using magic to see in the dark. Where was he? Probably in the thro—

"Mason!" I heard Pie yell as I crashed through the large stain glass window and fell two stories down onto the hard stone ground outside.

I lay there. I broke almost every single bone in my body when I collided with the ground. However, I felt power rushing through my body, quickly healing me as fast as it could. The pain slowly slipped away, and I got back on my feet.

Pie jumped out the window, vanished into thin air, and reappeared next to me. "He's inside. Get ready for a fight."

"Do you think I need my guardian's uniform for this?" I asked.

"Nah, your bow won't hurt him anyway," Pie said.

"True, but I got the stone." I pulled the wisdom stone from my pocket, and it instantly transformed into a bow with one arrow.

"Only one?! You better not miss, bro," Pie told me as we both stared up at the hole in the window.

My heart raced as we waited for Qadir to appear.

"Do I ever miss?" I asked with a smug grin.

"Well, there was that one time when you al—" he began, but I cut him off.

"Shut up," I hissed.

"Sorry," he muttered.

"There!" I shouted as Qadir stepped to the hole in the window and into our view.

"Hi, Dad!" Pie yelled.

I just looked at him like he was stupid and ignored it. I aimed the arrow at Qadir, but before I could shoot, he vanished and appeared a few feet in front of us. Bridget was next to him, trapped in an hour glass as sand poured down on her.

"Bridget?" I questioned quietly.

"Let her go!" Pie instantly yelled. He never sounded so angry before.

"Surrender to me, Mason, or she dies," Qadir threatened.

Panic. That's what I was feeling right now. How did he get Bridget? She was going to suffocate in there if I didn't do something about it. I looked around as the unique purple sky of Sariah was getting darker, which meant time was running out. I had to do something, or many people would die. I knew one thing for sure. Bridget wouldn't want me to surrender. Without hesitation, I whipped my hand in front of me and made Qadir go flying into through the castle wall, leaving a large gaping hole through it.

"Pie! Try to get Bridget out while I will hold him off!" I told him and went after Qadir.

Courage and power flooded me. Walking through the giant hole in the wall that I had just created, I stood over Qadir and kicked him ferociously before he could get back on his feet. I made the wisdom stone transform into sword and went after him again. I felt so much rage. It was as if I weren't really myself. I felt power and invincibility.

Qadir vanished before my eyes, and suddenly, multiple copies of him appeared around me. I snarled in anger as I tried to figure out which one was the real Qadir, standing in battle form just in case anything attacked. I knew if I could fight him off easily with the help of the Twilight, but I knew the more I used it, the easier it would be for my mind to get corrupted again. I was so tempted to use it, and only a small feeling kept me from not summoning Twilight creatures.

"You're a coward, Qadir! Face me!" I yelled.

Instantly, all the copies laughed. The hideous taunting snickering echoed around the room and drove me crazy. I literally could feel myself getting angrier and angrier. I let out a loud scream of rage, and all the copies burst into flames but vanished just after. I sneered when the ground beneath me began to shake, and the ceiling of the castle began to cave in. I shot a looked toward Pie who was still desperately trying to free Bridget. Luckily, he saw the castle coming down on us, so right before I was crushed, I saw him put a force field around them to protect them. I, however, was too occupied, making sure they would be okay. I was caught under a bunch of ruins.

Agony filled me as I lay under the pile of rocks unable to move. I had to get out. I closed my eyes and concentrated the best I could. With a bright flash, the rocks blasted off of me, and I lay there gasping for air. Qadir stood above me shortly after. I just glared as I waited for my body to heal itself.

"You know, my offer still stands. Join me. Rule the entire world with me like we always wanted," he said.

"I never wanted that," I said and got on my feet. I reached for the sword, but I had lost it. I must've lost it when the ceiling came crashing down on us. I looked around in panic, and Qadir made me go flying out into the courtyard. Smashing my skull against the stone court, I blacked out for a second or two. I glanced back over to Bridget and Pie. The hour glass still intact with Bridget inside, the sand was up to her neck as Pie tried his hardest to smash the glass.

My head healed quickly. It probably would've taken longer if I wasn't trained to heal faster than the other gods did. Most of my childhood, Alash would torture me to make me stronger, to make me the perfect weapon. I sat up and grew very confused when I saw that I was no longer in the courtyard of Qadir's castle. I was on a giant chessboard. There were no walls, and only darkness surrounded me. What was going on?

"Qadir?!" I yelled. My voice made me sound scared, and honestly, I was a little. I was alone. I hated being alone. "Qadir?!" I shouted again, sounding even more frightened.

"You're afraid," Qadir spoke from behind me. I felt him right up to my ear, whispering to me. "And you call out my name. What does that tell you?"

I spun around and tried to blast him away from me. However, when I turned around, he wasn't there. I was getting sick of his tricks. Qadir's famous laughter chimed around me once again as I began to run down the chessboard, hoping to escape. But the board never seemed to end. I got more frustrated and stopped. I sighed and tried to figure out what was happening when out of nowhere, I went flying and rammed into a tree. That's when I realized I was still in the courtyard. Qadir had made an illusion to confuse me. I took a deep breath. I needed to stop worrying about Qadir and find that celestial weapon.

"Had enough yet?" Qadir asked and kneeled down in front of me. He grabbed me by the throat and pinned me to the ground. Then he grabbed me by the wrists and held me down like that. "Consider this a defeat. I won't kill you, but I own you now forever."

The sound of glass shattering came from the distance. I didn't pay much attention to it because I had a psychopath on top of me. I struggled the best I could, but his grip was strong. This was it. The only thing I could do now was use the Twilight...no matter what it would do to me. I began to concentrate wishing that I didn't have to do this. I opened my palm to begin the spell to let the Twilight loose on Qadir.

Qadir leaned in closer to my face. "Finally, I have yo—" He immediately stopped when a blade was driven through his heart. The blade was just inches away from piercing me was well. Qadir let go of me and dropped to the ground. Once he dropped, I saw Pie standing there in tears as he pulled the sword out of his father's back.

I stared at him in shock. "Oh, gods...Pie..." I mumbled sadly. I never thought Pie would ever do this.

He didn't even look at me. Bridget stood behind him shocked herself. Pie kneeled down by Qadir as a black cloud of smoke floated out of Qadir's eyes and over to me, circling around my arm. I opened my palm again and absorbed it. It was the Twilight creature I had put inside Qadir. Qadir was no longer under my corruption, but it was too late for him. Qadir lay here gasping for air with Pie beside him, crying. Qadir reached his hand out to his son, and Pie took it.

"I-I...I am so s-sorry," Qadir said weakly to Pie as tears poured from his eyes.

Pie hugged his father and sobbed. "It's okay, Dad," he uttered the best he could.

That's when I felt it. I felt Qadir die. I had that ability to feel the soul leave a body, being the son of the death god.

Qadir was dead. The Realms was safe.

CHAPTER SEVENTEEN:

In the dark

I still couldn't believe what happened. I couldn't believe Qadir was gone. The terror was over, and for now, I had nothing to worry about. Bridget, Pie, and I took the time to bury Qadir for Pie of course. If it was up to me, I would've let him rot there. Pie wasn't crying as much as before. I wish he never had to kill his own father. I should've done it, but I wasn't strong enough. I admired Pie greatly. He was the one who saved the Realms even if he had to pay greatly for it.

Eventually, we went back to the Sanctuary. Qadir's soldiers never made it to the kingdom. My mother's army of high elves killed them before they could reach us. The soldiers didn't stand a chance against those tall flamboyant and graceful species. Once the news of Qadir was announced, the entire Realms rejoiced, and the celebrations began.

"So, guess what?" Bridget said as we sat on the balcony, watching the festival beneath us. The full moon shining bright, and everything was so joyful. It was a nice feeling.

"What?" I questioned.

"Don't freak out," she told me and took a deep breath. "I...have a boyfriend."

I looked at her surprised and smiled. "Who?"

"Pie" She smiled, blushing a bit.

"Yes! I've been waiting for you two to start dating," I confessed.

"What?! You have?" she questioned.

"Yep." I smirked. "I'm so happy for you. Pie is a great guy."

"Thanks. Griffin didn't take it too well when I told him," she said.

"What did he do?" I asked.

Bridget sighed, "He didn't say anything. He just looked at me like I was stupid and walked off with Lexi."

"Sounds like something he'd do," I said.

"Yeah." She pouted.

I looked back down at the people and smiled. I felt so relieved that there was peace again.

"Mason..." Matt said from behind us.

"What?" I turned to look at him.

"The Sonyin Sorcerers request your presence at Kule Palace," he told me.

"Now?" I wondered.

He just nodded.

I looked at Bridget. "You wanna come?"

"Am I even allowed to?" she asked.

I shrugged. "If they don't want you there, they'll just ask you to leave the council room."

"Okay, then. I'll go." She smiled.

"Okay, cool," I said and walked off, expecting

Bridget to follow.

We headed downstairs. Griffin, Lexi, and Pie were waiting for us.

"Hey." I smiled at them.

Lexi smiled back. Griffin was too busy glaring at Pie as he went over and kissed Bridget.

"You ready to go?" Lexi asked. "We can get there faster with the warpstone Max gave you."

"Okay, sounds good," I said and gripped the stone.

"Mason, wait!" Susalea shouted as she ran down the hall over to me. "Before you go, I have something urgent I must speak with you about."

"It can't wait?" I questioned, letting go of the stone around my neck.

She shook her head. "It's waited long enough."

I looked back at my friends and sighed, "Okay, we'll go in a second. Hold on," I told them and walked off with Susalea. "What is it?"

"Look. While you were gone in Leadville, something happened with Caroline," Susalea began. "In fact, it happened a month before you vanished. She was going to tell you, but you left."

"What are you talking about?" I was so confused.

"I am only telling you this now because Qadir is gone, which means it might be safe for you to meet him," Susalea said.

"Meet who?" I asked sternly.

"Caroline was a month pregnant before you left for a year and had a baby while you were gone. We covered it up," Susalea stated.

My eyes widened. I just stared at her in utter shock.

"Mason?" She waved her hand in front of my

face to check if I was still with her.

"A b-baby… I'm a father?" I stammered.

She nodded. "Yeah, his name is Peter," Susalea then told me. "We gave him to a kind family. Caroline was scared that Qadir would try to kill him."

"He's still not safe," I told her. "Oh, gods… I can't have a kid. He'll die."

"So, you don't want to meet him?" she asked.

"I can't get near him. With my father still around, who the hell knows what will happen in the future? I can't risk him dying!" I panicked.

"It's still a good idea for you to know about him," she said. "He lives in Marry Villa if you want to meet him. He lives with the blacksmith and his wife," Susalea told me and walked off.

I stood there trying to take the news. *I had a son…I had a child!* I was a father, but even if I wanted to, which I honestly sort of didn't, I couldn't be in his life. He was better off without me. I had too many enemies. I took a deep breath and began to walk back to my friends as they were waiting for me patiently.

I went over to them and sighed, "Okay, let's get out of here."

"You okay? You look like you saw a ghost," Griffin commented.

"I'm fine," I told him and grasped the warpstone. "Everyone, take each other's hands."

Everyone held hands, and we teleported away, appearing in front of Kule Palace. Kule Palace was as tall as a skyscraper. It looked like a giant castle made out of pure gold. For all I knew, it really was gold. The gates opened as soon as we approached, but no guards stood by them. They just opened on their own.

"So, do we just walk in?" Bridget asked.

"I think so," I said.

"Well, how else would we get inside?" Griffin sassed and entered the Palace.

We all followed him, heading down the main hall and toward the large golden doors to the throne room where all the gods waited for us. Entering the throne room took a lot of courage. I knew they all wanted me dead. They knew that I was the one who locked them up and was the one who started all the conflict in the Realms to begin with. I expected no mercy.

We all stood before Castrin and the rest of the Sonyin Sorcerers, my father being one of them. I avoided eye contact with him. There were thirteen thrones with only two empty, my mother and Qadir's. Castrin sat in the middle with his brother, Asa, god of the sea, and Valentine, Castrin's wife, goddess of the heavens and skies sat beside him. Then there was my father, Alash, god of death, and Katerina, goddess of misery—she and I had an odd friendship. Since our powers were the most alike, we kind of got along really well, but we also hated each other because we made each other feel what we made others feel. It's confusing. They were all here. Alaric, God of war, hunt, and strategy. Dawn, God of music. Damon, god of love. Bell Fire, god of joy. Grace, Goddess of wisdom. Then Samantha, goddess of thieves, Bridget and Griffin's mother.

I had no idea where my mother was, and Qadir was dead, so this was the council of the Sonyin sorcerers at the moment. All of them were billions of years old. I would hate to be alive for so long. Life would lose meaning, but since I was immortal myself, who knows how long I'd be alive? Castrin looked unamused as he usually did. I only saw him smile once before. He was always so serious. Castrin had short, black wavy hair, blue eyes, and pale skin. He wore a black suit with no tie and had a pocket watch in his blazer pocket. Probably because he was the god of time.

"Pippin, step forward," Castrin ordered.

Pie did what Castrin said and stepped a bit closer to the gods. Bridget, Lexi, Griffin, and I stayed quiet.

"Your father, Qadir, is no longer able to be the Sonyin sorcerers of Mischief. The council of the Sonyin would like you to take his position," Castrin said with his rich, baritone voice. "Do you accept?"

Pie looked toward the ground sadly and nodded. "Yes, I accept."

I knew he never wanted this day to come.

"Good. You may take a seat then," Castrin told him and gestured to Qadir's old throne.

Pie walked over and sat down. Castrin then shot his gaze upon me, and my heart began to race. I was going to get it.

"Mason, step forward," he ordered me.

I shook my head no. "I like where I'm standing."

He gave me a cold glare. "I am not joking around, Mason. Stop with your idiotic sass, and step forward," he sounded very pissed.

I stepped forward hesitantly, taking a deep breath and preparing to get yelled at.

"Everyone here knows that you were the cause of all of this bloodshed. You locked us all away for over a year," Castrin began. "You cannot control your powers. You're a threat to the Realms, so we have all voted for you to be exterminated."

My eyes widened. I had been sentenced to death.

"No! Please don't kill my brother," Lexi spoke

out, stepping in front of me.

"He has his power back. He will lose his mind again and kill everyone," Castrin stated. "He's a danger to our world."

"Brother, if I may cut in... I have an idea," My father spoke with a fake smile planted on his face. "Mason only lost control when you allowed King Matthew to take him from me."

"Where are you going with this?" Castrin asked Alash.

"Whatever it is, it can't be good," Griffin stated and stepped next to me.

"Let me take Mason back. I kept him under control. He never hurt anyone when he was with me in my kingdom," Alash said.

I looked at Castrin with my face creamed panic. "Kill me," I said. "Kill me please."

"You can't allow Alash to take Mason back. He will hurt him," Griffin told them.

"Badly. He will hurt Mason in inhumane ways," Bridget chimed in.

Castrin kept quiet and thought for a moment.

"Let's take a vote," Damon, the god of love, suggested.

"Yeah, let's take a vote," Pie said.

"Okay, all in favor of sparing Mason Gray's life and allowing him to walk free, raise your hand," Castrin said, and only Pie and Katerina raised their hands. I was screwed either way now. "All right, now if you think we should execute Mason, please raise your hand." Only a few, three or four at the most, sorcerers raised their hands, which I was hoping more would because that meant the majority was going to side with my father. "Raise your hand if you think we should let

Alash take care of him."

The rest of the gods who didn't vote before raised their hands. My heart sank. I was being thrown back in the hands of my abusive father.

Suddenly, some of my father's guards entered and grabbed me. I fought them back, and Bridget and Griffin began to help me when we all froze unable to move.

"Our word is final!" Castrin yelled.

Alash stood and walked toward the doors. His guards grabbed me and dragged me off. I couldn't fight anymore nor could Bridget or Griffin. They stood there frozen, watching me leave.

"Mason!" Lexi cried. "Please don't let Alash take him!" she begged the sorcerers, and they just sat there not caring. She almost ran after me; however, Alaric held her back, and soon, I exited the throne room with my father.

"What are you planning to do to me?" I asked my father.

He stopped, and so did the guards and me. He turned around, snapped his fingers, and I was knocked out cold. I wasn't sure how long I was out. By now, I was sure we had reached my father's kingdom, Morena, the Hell of the Realms. It definitely was my hell. I awoke inside the same hole in the ground that I had been in my dream where I killed Lexi. My arms were shackled to the stone walls surrounding me. I looked up, and Alash stood at the top, smirking down at me.

"It'll be just like old times, Mason," he said down to me and walked off, letting the guards seal the door.

Soon, I was surrounded by darkness. I couldn't see anything. I tried to stand up the best I could and began to try to break out, but the chains were made of diamond. Sonyin gods couldn't break diamond.

"Let me out!" I yelled, panicking. I was so afraid. I couldn't relive what I had endured in the past. "Let me out of here!" I screamed as loud as I could, but nothing. He just left me to rot until he decided to come to torture me.

Tears poured from my eyes, and I sat down, hugging myself. I was over. This was my ending. He was going to destroy me, and there was nothing I could do about it.

ABOUT THE AUTHOR

Autumn A. Hutchings is an author, living in Castle Rock, Colorado. She has been working on Broken Realm since she was in the 8th grade. Her only hope for the future is that her books become loved by everyone across the world. She wants to move to Leadville, Colorado to be closer to her stories. Autumn has a few hobbies, which include writing, cosplaying, and acting. She loves talking to her fans and appreciates them all very much.

Autumn is a member of the Church of Jesus Christ of Latter-day Saints and has been all her life. She is currently attending DC Oakes high school, working on the last book of the Broken Realm series, and has many more series planned. She wants to be a writer as her profession but could see herself being an actor on the side.